I know a bit about magical worlds, and it certainly takes a very special kind of writer to create a fantasy so convincing and immersive that I almost believe it's real. In *The Boy Who Went Magic*, A. P. Winter has achieved this in spades. His remarkable story is laced with ancient magic, immediate danger and irresistibly fantastic inventions. Now I'm desperate for some mechanical legs . . . (you'll find out!).

BARRY CUNNINGHAM
Publisher
Chicken House

The Boy
WHO WENT
Magic

A. P. WINTER

Chicken House

2 Palmer Street, Frome, Somerset BA11 1DS

A. P. Winter has asserted his right under the Copyright, Designs and Patents Act 1988
to be identified as the author of this work.

Cover and interior design by Steve Wells
Cover illustration by Manuel Sumberac
Typeset by Dorchester Typesetting Group Ltd
Printed and bound in Great Britain by CPI Group (UK) Ltd, Croydon CR0 4YY

The paper used in this Chicken House book is made from wood grown in sustainable forests.

1 3 5 7 9 10 8 6 4 2

British Library Cataloguing in Publication data available.

PB ISBN 978-1-910655-09-2
eISBN 978-1-911077-41-1

Prologue

....

The carriage driver struck a match with a sharp snap and the lantern sprang to life. A dark, foggy stretch of the city lay ahead. 'You'll excuse the delay, sir,' said the driver, to a man sitting beside him in a hooded cloak. 'These narrow ways can be dangerous at this hour.'

The man in the cloak nodded. His hood obscured his face, but the restless movement of his head showed his unease. His hand gripped a sword at his belt.

Both men seemed to expect trouble. The horses stamped their feet and snorted. The reins jangled as the driver urged them onwards.

The small boy watched the men closely from the seat behind, clutching his ragged coat against the cold. He felt confused and shaken. He couldn't remember how he had got there, only that he had been afraid, and that the man in the cloak had saved him. Everything else was a blur.

The driver gestured to the boy. 'I wouldn't want him to be scared of the darkness,' he said, in a voice that betrayed his own fears. The lantern bobbed over their heads as the carriage approached a set of tall iron gates. 'Is this the place, sir?' said the driver. 'The school?'

The man in the cloak gave a muffled reply.

The driver slowed the horses. 'I suppose he's a runaway?' he said. He gestured towards the boy. 'He doesn't look like your typical troublemaker though, does he?'

'What business is that of yours?' said the man.

The driver looked nervous. 'Forgive me, sir. I just meant, I thought that you looked like a lawman. I'm right, aren't I? Did he run away from the place?'

The man in the cloak didn't reply. He passed the driver some money, and then lifted the small child down from the seat. They walked together to the school gates.

The carriage drove away.

'It's all right,' said the man in the cloak. 'They'll look after you here.'

The child didn't reply.

The man in the cloak looked around suddenly at the tramp of approaching footsteps. They sounded like heavy boots. The man took the child's arm and led him into the shadows beside the gate. A group of soldiers appeared from around the corner. They were wearing tall hats and long-tailed coats, and they had their swords drawn. They were searching for someone.

'Stay together,' said the leader of the group, waving his sword. 'Search every possible corner.'

The boy felt a chill of fear.

'Stay low,' whispered the cloaked man. 'And stay in the shadows.'

The child did as he was told, but his hands were shaking.

The men cast their lanterns over the dark street and the puddles shone like glass. The child and the man in the cloak crouched further into the shadows. There was only a thin alcove to hide them from sight. It was too late to run. The men were coming closer.

'Who are we even chasing?' whispered one of the soldiers.

'Quiet there,' snapped the leader. 'Stay alert.'

'But sir,' chimed in another man, as he peered into the alleyways. 'How are we supposed to find someone, in a city full of people, if we don't know what they look like?'

The leader seemed as if he was about to give a stern reply, when the outline of a man appeared through the fog. All the soldiers turned in alarm.

The child stared at the new apparition, unsure of what to expect. He felt instinctively afraid – more afraid than he was of the soldiers. He struggled not to make a sound.

'Who goes there?' demanded the leader.

The outline loomed closer. It was clear that whoever was approaching wasn't daunted by the challenge. 'Do you not know your own prince?' said a harsh voice.

The lead soldier shrank back in obvious alarm. 'Prince Voss, Your Highness,' he stammered. 'Please forgive me. We did not know that you had joined the search . . .'

Voss was already striding past the man. The prince was tall and strong, and wore a long dark coat with a large pistol on his belt. In his gloved hand he held a glittering sword. He glared around the street. 'Have you seen anyone suspicious?' he said, in a deep, rasping tone.

'No, sir. No sign of disturbance.'

The prince stood frozen for a moment. The soldiers seemed too frightened to speak. 'No sign,' muttered the prince. He picked up a loose cobble from the street, and clenched it in his grasp. There was a loud crack and the cobble fell as dust from his fingers.

The men looked at one another in horror.

'Traitors,' hissed Voss.

The nearest solider flinched. 'I beg your pardon, Your Highness?'

'We are hunting traitors,' said Voss. He pointed to the man who had been asking questions about the search. 'There is a child belonging to a house of traitors, guilty of keeping secrets from the crown – guilty of involvement in the ancient crime of magic.' He patted the dust from his hand, and glared at the men around him. 'I need it found,' he hissed.

The child felt another shudder of fear.

The prince walked towards their hiding place, and the man in the cloak put his hand on his sword. But the prince moved on without pause. His footsteps faded.

The small boy's eyes grew accustomed to the darkness. He could see the soldiers' faces. They were visibly shaken, but that didn't stop them whispering to one another

'The prince is as mad as they say,' said one of the men.

'All the royals are,' muttered another.

'How did he crush a stone like that?'

'I heard he has a false hand.'

'Really?'

'I heard he chopped off the real one himself.'

Their leader seemed too shocked to reproach them. He placed his hand against a wall for support, and let out a deep breath. 'Thank goodness he's gone,' he said.

A soldier cleared his throat. 'Did he mean what he said, sir?'

'About what?' said the leader.

'I mean, that the traitors used, well . . . magic.'

The soldiers looked uneasily at one another. The word *magic* seemed to make them even more nervous. The leader hesitated for a moment before he replied. 'You should know better than to pay attention to things like that,' he said. 'Every soldier in Penvellyn knows that magic is just a fairy tale. Swords and pistols are the only real power. Now, let's finish this sweep.'

With his speech finished he drew himself up importantly, and led the men around the next corner of the street. Their voices faded into the night.

The cloaked man shook his head. 'Fairy tales,' he muttered.

He helped the child up, and stood facing the school gateway. There was a heavy lock around the bars. The man took a strange-looking key from his pocket and turned the mechanism.

The gate opened with a dull clank, and they walked into the deserted courtyard of the school. The building was typical of the Penvellyn style. There were heavy stone pillars supporting the protruding upper floors. The windows rose into pointed arches. The child didn't like the place. He shuddered as the man led him up the stone steps and hammered on the wooden door.

After a moment, they heard footsteps.

'What is it?' said a muffled voice.

'Legal business,' said the cloaked man.

'The law?' said the man on the other side of the door. He opened the lock hurriedly to reveal a worried-looking face, with a thin grey beard. 'You'll forgive me for asking, sir – but what business does the law have with us, at this time of night? We haven't reported any crime.'

The cloaked man stepped inside, and the child followed. A dim light shone from a candle holder on a desk across the room. The tall ceiling disappeared in darkness.

'I need you to look after this child.'

The bearded man frowned. 'This child?' he said. 'He looks too young to begin proper schooling. Surely he would be better placed with a nanny?'

The small boy looked around nervously. There was a stuffed owl on a plinth in a recess beside the door and a large painting of a stern old man wearing a crown.

'Are you his father?' asked the bearded man.

The man in the cloak shook his head. 'He doesn't have any parents,' he said. 'He was living as an urchin, out in the scrap heaps in the southern district. He has nothing.'

The bearded man made a disgusted face. 'I'm afraid we don't involve ourselves in matters of charity,' he said. 'Oneiros School is a respectable institution, after all.'

The man in the cloak pulled out a purse from his belt and passed it over. 'That will be enough to see him through the first years, I believe. I'll bring the rest soon.'

'The rest?'

'For his complete schooling,' said the man in the cloak. 'I want him to be looked after. And I don't want you to make any reference to his former life, you understand?'

The bearded man was distracted for a moment by the contents of the purse. He took out a gold coin with a look of wonder. 'This is . . . very generous,' he said.

'You understand my terms?'

'Oh yes, yes,' said the bearded man. 'He'll be well looked after. The best education. We don't just teach mathematics and spelling here. Every subject a child needs in the modern world – navigation, sword fighting, amphor engineering, even the occasional horse-riding class. We can send you reports on his progress at whatever interval works best for you.'

'No,' said the man in the cloak. 'I won't be in communication with him again, I'm afraid, unless I find that there is some problem with the way he is being schooled.' He spoke the words softly, but there was a coldness to his voice that suggested he was used to being obeyed.

'Of course,' said the bearded man. He hurriedly took a large book from the desk, and began to talk about a receipt of payment, and special instructions for the child's induction.

The small boy began to cry. He could see now that the man in the cloak was leaving him in this strange place, with this strange man.

'It's all right,' said the man in the cloak. 'You'll be safe here.'

The bearded man looked up from his writing. He sneered at the child and shook his head. 'We will soon teach him to toughen up, sir,' he said. 'What name should I enter for him?'

The man in the cloak muttered something the child didn't catch. It was obvious that he wasn't happy with the school man. He whispered: 'Do you remember your name?'

The boy shook his head and sniffed.

'Well, we'll have to enter a name for him,' said the school man. 'Perhaps a plain and simple choice. It makes the child humble.'

'What would you recommend?' said the cloaked man curtly.

'All things considered, I would recommend Bert. And we have a lack of family names beginning with "R".' He snorted. 'I suppose we could make him Bert Rumsey.'

'Fine,' said the man in the cloak. He stood up straight, and looked towards the door. 'I'm afraid I have to leave on other business. Take good care of him.'

'Don't,' said the small child. He caught hold of the man's cloak.

The man looked down.

'It's scary here,' said the boy.

The man in the cloak froze. His hood still obscured his face. He knelt and hugged the boy. 'It won't always be scary,' he said. 'I promise.' He stood up quickly and strode towards the door, pulling his cloak tighter. The door opened and closed, and he was gone.

Chapter 1

Bert stood watching the crowds gather inside the entrance of Penvellyn National Museum. A procession of horse-drawn carriages dropped off important-looking people in tall hats as a sightseeing airship passed overhead. The voice of the tour guide carried down to the street: '*Below you'll see a group of children waiting for the first public opening. How lucky they must feel. King Eldred himself sanctioned the exhibit only yesterday, along with the handsome Prince Voss . . .*' The wind rose, and the rest of the commentary was lost to the noise of the street.

Bert shook his head. He wasn't feeling especially lucky. Ten years had passed since his arrival at the school. He was thirteen, tall and stern, and carried himself almost like an adult. But he still found the memory of that night creeping into his thoughts from time to time, making him feel like a small child again.

His schoolmates were whispering to one another about the new exhibition. All they knew for certain was that it was about the old land of Ferenor – and that they were missing classes for it. A day off school was exciting enough in itself, even without the added mystery.

'Hey, Bert,' said a boy named Freston.

'What?' said Bert, immediately on his guard.

'Maybe there'll be something *magical*.' Freston wiggled his fingers in the air as he spoke, and pulled a face. A few of the other children sniggered.

Bert chose not to reply.

'Didn't you say you were going to be an adventurer?' said Freston.

'Maybe, when I was six,' said Bert. He moved away from Freston and his group of cronies and tried to make himself inconspicuous.

A girl called Garnet looked his way and smiled. She was one of the most popular people in his class, which meant she was basically his opposite. She never spoke to him.

He was taken aback for a moment.

'How's it going?' she said.

Bert blinked. 'I – I'm fine, how are you?'

Garnet frowned and looked past him.

Bert realized that she wasn't talking to him at all, but a girl who was standing over his shoulder. He winced and looked at his feet. It was sort of funny, in a way. But in another way, it made him want to crawl into a hole in the ground and never speak again. He should have known better, he supposed. The important children weren't accustomed to mixing with orphans.

'Right, children,' said Mr Fitzroy, their teacher. He was an impatient man, with a small moustache and an uneasy way of glancing at people. 'Some of you may be wondering why we have come to this place. Well, let me tell you – we have not cancelled today's scheduled sword fighting exams and travelled across town by omnibus without good reason. What you are about to see today, as some of the first visitors to this exhibition, will form a fundamental part of your education. It will help dismiss any fairy tale notions you might have about magic for good.'

Bert winced. *Fairy tale notions?* He thought again of that night, and the voice of the man in the cloak. Sometimes he wondered if it was just a bad dream. He sensed the other children watching him. Garnet whispered something to her friends, and the sniggering began all over again.

'Let us find our tour guide,' said Mr Fitzroy. He put

his cane under his arm, and led them into a spacious room where a large window made reflections on the marble floor. There was a statue nearby that showed King Eldred handing over a sword to the first prime minister. The plaque underneath read: KING ELDRED HANDS THE POWER OF GOVERNANCE TO THE PEOPLE. The date on the plaque was thirty years ago. Bert studied the king's face. The smile didn't seem very sincere.

They passed under a sign that proclaimed: THE MYTH OF MAGIC: HOW MODERN STUDY HAS EXPOSED THE FRAUD OF FERENOR. Bert felt hollow inside. He couldn't admit it openly, but he still possessed a quiet appreciation for the tales of Ferenor – the battles, mages, knights and ghosts. It had given him comfort whenever he looked out on the bustle of Penvellyn City, with its smoke stacks and carriage-filled streets, or whenever he felt the dreariness of school life getting him down.

It felt good to imagine something magical.

The children had already begun to laugh at the exhibits. Freston was pulling a face and pointing at a picture on the wall. The picture showed a man conjuring fire out of the ground and fighting a group of soldiers with his bare hands. The scene looked ridiculous, but that was clearly the idea. 'Look at him,' said Freston, crossing his eyes. 'He's gone magic.'

The children giggled until Mr Fitzroy silenced them.

Bert was the only one who wasn't amused. 'Going magic' was common slang amongst the school children for anyone who didn't fit in with the crowd. It was an insult that Bert was more than familiar with.

'Is this who you wanted to be when you were little, Bert?' whispered Freston, while Mr Fitzroy was busy consulting a map on the opposite wall. 'Something wizardy?'

'Very funny,' said Bert. He looked at the notice beside the picture.

The delusion of magic relied on a preposterous belief in warriors called mages. These mages were supposed to live in the land of Ferenor, which fell into ruin over two hundred years ago. It was said that they could move faster than any normal person, make machines that worked forever, perform huge feats of strength, and draw energy out of nowhere . . . does that sound real to you?

Bert sighed. 'Not when you put it like that,' he muttered.

'Where is that guide?' said Mr Fitzroy. 'Excuse me!'

A tall, broad-shouldered man who'd been crossing the room checked his step and turned to face them. He was wearing a black hat and an academic cape. 'Yes?' he said.

'Err . . . we were waiting . . .' said Mr Fitzroy nervously. He seemed unwilling to address the man directly, and

Bert could see why. There was something fierce in the tall man's gaze.

'Waiting for what?' said the tall man.

'For the tour,' said Mr Fitzroy.

'Oh,' said the tall man. He looked down at his attire, as if only just noticing it for the first time. 'Then I suppose you're waiting for me.' He cleared his throat. 'I'm afraid the tour will be quite brief, children, but feel free to ask questions as we go. You may call me Professor.' Without any further introduction, he turned his back and strode into the next exhibition room.

'Err . . . keep up, children,' said Mr Fitzroy.

Bert could sense that there was something strange about the Professor, but he couldn't put his finger on what exactly – perhaps it was that the man didn't quite fit his uniform. His beard and the heavy tread of his stride didn't seem particularly scholarly either.

'Right,' said the Professor, waving to some cabinets as they passed. 'This is the domestic section, I suppose. You'll see most of it is just old rags. Not very interesting.'

Mr Fitzroy opened his mouth to protest, but the Professor was already hurrying them towards the next room. At the doorway, Bert noticed the Professor stop and listen for a moment before entering. He had the uncomfortable feeling that the man was up to something, but he quickly forgot his misgivings as the class entered the next section and were met with a large model of an adventuring airship in the centre of the room – just like Bert had seen in his school books.

The Professor folded his arms and nodded appreciatively. 'That's a fine-looking ship,' he said. 'This is how we retrieve artefacts from the ruins of Ferenor,' he explained. 'It's too dangerous to cross by sea, but with an airship you can fly over, or fight off, the worst of the perils.'

Freston put his hand up. 'Why is it dangerous?' he asked. He was clearly trying to show off. 'I thought there weren't any native people in Ferenor – not for over two hundred years. The people there weren't clever enough to survive, and invent machines and things, like us . . .'

'Well, there might not be any *native* people,' interrupted the Professor. 'But there are pirates that travel across from our own land, and monsters, and ghosts if you're unlucky.'

Some of the children laughed nervously. They seemed to think that the Professor was joking, but Bert wasn't so sure. He caught a strange look of pride in the man's eyes.

'Of course,' said the Professor, 'anyone who wants to travel there must get permission from the government, and hand over any treasure or artefacts that they find to the government for study. So, all in all it's not a very profitable business.' He smiled grimly. 'Unless you're a pirate, of course. Then you can sell your treasures on the black market for a tidy sum.'

The children laughed again.

'Excuse me,' said My Fitzroy.

'Yes?' said the Professor.

'Shouldn't we be focusing on the real point of the exhibition?'

'The real point?'

'Yes.'

The Professor scratched his nose. 'And what would that be?'

Mr Fitzroy stood up straight and raised his chin indignantly. 'That this power called "magic" is merely a myth – passed down by foolish generations. Hasn't that now been proved?'

'Oh,' said the Professor. 'I see. I suppose looking at the pots and pulleys and rags of this exhibit you might imagine that the people of Ferenor never did anything particularly interesting. Especially not compared to our modern amphor engines and gunpowder and adventuring airships. I believe that is the "point" of the exhibition, as you understand it?'

'Precisely,' said Mr Fitzroy. He smiled weakly. 'So . . .?'

'Well, I'm going to show you all something that isn't included in the official tour,' said the Professor. 'Then you can decide for yourselves.' He headed to a door in the corner of the room, and took a set of keys from his pocket. There was a notice beside it that read: No Entry, Under Pain of Death, By Order of the Royal Crown. The Professor tried several keys before it unlocked. 'After you,' he said, ushering the children and the teacher inside, and locking the door behind them.

'I wasn't told about this,' said Mr Fitzroy.

'Then you'll enjoy the surprise,' said the Professor. He led them down a dark staircase and through a heavy iron door which opened into a long basement room. The room was lined with shelves and drawers containing all sorts of strange oddities: golden mechanisms which had no purpose that Bert could fathom; suits of armour – or what appeared to be suits of armour – with fierce faces sculpted into them; oddly shaped weapons covered in strange writing. A whole wall was devoted to curious-looking lanterns with gigantic glass bulbs, and there was a rack of what seemed to be metal hands

Bert crossed the room slowly, feeling more confused with every step.

'Hello,' said a strange voice.

Bert glanced around. He was alert for some trick from Freston, and wary of making the same mistake as when he thought Garnet was speaking to him. He shook his head.

'Hello?' said the voice again.

'Can anyone hear that?' asked Bert.

The other children didn't acknowledge him. They huddled together nervously as the Professor led them towards a set of cabinets that housed a life-size metal man.

Suddenly, Bert's gaze was drawn to a shiny object standing inside a glass cabinet. Without thinking, he stepped away from his classmates and put his fingers against the glass. Inside the cabinet was a mirror with a gold and silver frame, and a strange shimmering quality. Its surface appeared more like a pool of water than a piece of glass, and the longer Bert stared into it, the less aware he felt of the room around him. He seemed almost to be floating above the ground. It was a pleasant sensation, and he felt annoyed when a smug voice broke into his reverie.

'Bert is trying to touch the exhibits.'

'Is that so?' said Mr Fitzroy. 'You will have detention, Bert.'

'Yes, sir,' said Bert. As he spoke he felt a wave of indignation. It seemed to grow from his toes and crackle through his mind. 'It's not fair,' he muttered. He turned away from the mirror, feeling deflated. But as he did so he felt the hairs stand up on his neck. He turned back and saw that something odd was happening. A blue light glittered over the mirror's surface.

The Professor approached. 'What's that?' he said.

'Nothing,' said Bert. 'I mean, I didn't do it.'

The mirror continued to glow.

'That's strange,' said the Professor. 'It's active.'

'What do you mean?' said Bert.

The children and their teacher took a step back, but the Professor stood with Bert, and placed his hand on the glass. 'Well, it looks like it could be worth something,' he said. 'You've obviously got a good eye for treasure hunting, young man.'

Bert smiled, but it occurred to him that the Professor didn't sound much like a museum guide. There was a greedy look in his eyes. 'What is it?' asked Bert.

The Professor frowned. 'I really don't know,' he said. 'But I'm afraid I don't have time for distractions.' He turned his back to the mirror. 'Now, where were we?' he muttered.

Bert sensed something odd in the air around him. The light of the mirror changed to a red glow, and he instinctively sensed danger. There wasn't time to hesitate.

'Look out!' He leapt forwards and shoved the Professor aside. There was a flash from the mirror. He heard a scream as pain shot through his body. The world seemed to grow suddenly dark. He felt himself drifting away.

Chapter 2

T he Professor was kneeling at Bert's side, apparently telling him to hold on – that he would be all right – to open his eyes. Bert was confused for a moment. He felt as if he was floating again.

'I'm right here,' he said, feeling dizzy. But the Professor showed no sign of hearing him. Bert looked down and felt a jolt of horror. His own body was lying on the floor, with its eyes closed and face blank. He was floating outside of himself, like a ghost.

He cried out in alarm, but again no one seemed to hear him.

Before he could think of what to do next, there was another flash from the mirror. A strange light surrounded him and drew him towards the glass.

He passed straight into the mirror's surface and emerged on the other side. A strong light filled his vision. He was in a different room. The ceiling was much higher, and there was a large tapestry on the wall bearing the crest of the royal family. He was floating in front of another mirror, the twin of the one in the museum. At the back of his mind he felt a twinge of understanding. The mirrors were connected. He had been pulled through some kind of portal.

A man in a white coat stood opposite him, staring at the mirror, but he didn't seem to notice Bert. Instead, he looked nervously around the room. He flinched at the sound of heavy footsteps approaching.

The door creaked open. Prince Voss's large frame stood silhouetted in the morning light. 'Why have you summoned me, Doctor?' he said. 'Has something happened?'

Bert was panicked by the sight of the prince. He tried desperately to turn around and get back to the museum. But the mirror held him in place.

'I think it's just an anomaly—' began the doctor.

'It's glowing,' interrupted the prince. His eyes lit up as he crossed the room, drawing closer to where Bert was frozen. 'I knew it would work if we gave it time.'

'We don't know that it is working,' said the doctor.

'Of course it is,' said the prince sharply. He stepped closer and placed his hand beside the mirror frame. 'Bring the crystal. We need to be ready to trap it.'

The doctor brought a small black crystal over to the mirror.

'Good,' said Voss. 'Now we just have to wait.'

Bert flinched. He didn't understand what the prince was talking about, but it sounded threatening. He worried that his position might be discovered after all.

Another minute passed, and nothing happened.

'Where is the spirit?' said Voss.

Bert was terrified. Voss stood with his arms behind his back, staring straight at the spot where he was floating. For a moment, Bert thought the man had seen him.

'Where is it, Doctor?' repeated the prince, threateningly.

'I – I don't know,' stammered the doctor. 'We did everything right. The mirror is active, we saw the light, we used the magnetism of the crystal. It should be here.'

Bert remained completely still, hardly daring to trust his invisibility. The energy of the mirror still seemed to surround him, keeping him from moving freely.

'I need this spirit,' said Prince Voss. 'I thought that you would understand by now just how critical it is to my plans. I thought you would avoid disappointing me.'

The doctor looked terrified. 'Your Highness,' he said. 'I have done everything I can. Surely you can't blame me if such outlandish rituals fail to give us the results you desire.'

The prince remained silent.

The doctor laughed uneasily. 'Sir, we are dealing with something that has never been proven to exist. I mean, to try to do magic, here, in the modern world . . .'

The prince suddenly grabbed the doctor and lifted him off his feet. The sleeve of the prince's coat shifted upwards, exposing a glint of metal. 'Does this feel real to you, Doctor?' said the prince. 'Does this seem like something from a fairy tale?'

The doctor was clearly too frightened to reply. The prince pulled him closer and took hold of his head with one hand, forcing him to look at the mirror.

'That is the difference between you and me, Doctor,' said the prince. 'You look at this object, and you only see the past.' He let the doctor drop, and strode over to the surface of the mirror, until he was standing face to face with Bert. 'I look into it, and I see the future,' he said.

'I understand, Your Highness,' said the doctor.

'Do you?' snapped Prince Voss. 'Do you understand how badly this country needs a real ruler again – with real power? You, more than anyone, Doctor, should know the lengths I will go to to make that happen. For thirty years, my family has been humiliated. We have no real authority any more. And still you disappoint me.' He raised his voice towards the door. 'Guards!'

The door opened and a pair of soldiers marched into the room.

'Take the doctor to Grimwater Prison,' said the prince.

'Yes, sir,' said the men.

'Why?' said the doctor, in a quivering voice.

'Because it is my wish,' said the prince. 'Perhaps a little time there will allow you to think of a solution, instead of blaming the gifts that I have suffered to bring before you.'

'You can't do this!' yelled the doctor. 'The government will hear about it. The quæstors will investigate you. You can't behave like this in the modern world.'

Voss gave a deep grunt of amusement. 'So I understand, Doctor. And that is precisely why I need your help – to make the world right again.'

Bert's head spun, and the room vanished in a blur of light. He suddenly felt the cold stone floor against his back, and drew a deep, welcome breath.

A hand shook Bert's shoulder. He gasped and looked around to find that he was back in the real world again, lying in front of the mirror with the Professor beside him. He wasn't sure how long he'd been oblivious, but he could tell that something bad had happened. The other children were shouting in alarm, and Mr Fitzroy was trying to gather them together.

'Are you all right?' said the Professor.

'I saw something,' said Bert. He blinked dizzily. 'I was in another place.'

'Right, well . . . that's interesting,' said the Professor. He seemed distracted. 'I'm afraid this isn't really going to plan. I didn't imagine they'd have such unstable artefacts.'

'How could a mirror do that?' asked Bert.

'It's happening again,' cried Freston from across the room.

Bert followed the boy's gaze to the life-size metal man. The mannequin gave a groan, then suddenly clenched its fists and hammered on the glass. Mr Fitzroy screamed along with the children. A golden mechanism spun off its shelf and cast a strange green light over the room. The children screamed again. One of the girls ran to the door and tried to open it, but it seemed to be locked. 'We can't get out,' she yelled. 'We're trapped in here.'

'Now, now everyone,' said the Professor. 'Let's try to remain calm.'

Bert was afraid. 'What's happening?' he said.

'We're having some problems,' said the Professor.

'Why did you lock us in here?'

The Professor was obviously uncomfortable with this line of questioning. 'There isn't much time to explain,' he said. 'I need to make sure you aren't suffering any side effects from that . . . thing.' He pointed to a row of shelves. 'Let's talk over here.'

The Professor helped him up and led him away from the other frightened children. Bert felt a sudden stinging sensation in his hand and looked down. A mark had appeared on his right palm. It looked like a burn. To his horror, it began to glow with red light. 'What on earth?' he said. .

The Professor took hold of his arm. 'Don't move.'

The light and noise in the room increased as more objects came to life. A glass bulb glowed and projected a map in the air, and a sword began to crackle with blue flames. The disturbance seemed to centre around where Bert and the Professor were standing. Then the lights dimmed, and everything fell still. The pain in Bert's hand faded. The glowing mark disappeared.

'What does it mean?' asked Bert. 'What was that?'

The Professor frowned. 'I'm not sure,' he said. He tore some cloth from his cape and tied it around Bert's hand. 'But I wouldn't worry yourself unnecessarily. There are lots of strange and wonderful things in this world. For now, you should take care of that burn.'

'It – it's stopped,' said a quavering voice from behind the shelves. 'We're saved.'

'Be on your guard,' said Mr Fitzroy.

Bert couldn't help feeling sorry for his terrified classmates.

'I should never have brought you down here,' muttered the Professor. He seemed to be talking to himself. 'But then they'd have noticed the guide was missing . . .'

Bert flexed his hand. 'But what caused all this?'

'Perhaps now isn't the time to discuss it,' said the Professor.

'Where is that guide?' yelled Mr Fitzroy, as he approached their hiding place. He was shaking with fear. He held out his cane. 'What kind of Professor are you?'

The Professor straightened. 'I'm not *a* Professor,' he said. 'I'm *the* Professor. Professor Goodrich Roberts. And I would suggest that you keep your mouth shut and go and stand with the other children. I do not appreciate the presence of eavesdroppers.'

Mr Fitzroy turned pale. '*The* Professor,' he said. 'You don't mean, the *pirate*?'

Some of the children gasped at the word pirate. Even Bert was shocked. He knew there was something odd about the Professor, but he hadn't expected anything so adventurous.

The Professor motioned for Bert to follow him further away from the others. He picked up a sword from a cabinet, turned to the metal suit of armour, and broke the case open. 'I need someone to give me a hand with this,' he said. 'I'm sorry – what's your name?'

'Bert.' He gave a glance to the opposite side of the room, where Mr Fitzroy and the other children were hovering quietly by the door. From the looks on their faces it was clear that they thought he was crazy for standing so close to a dangerous, wanted man.

'Well, Bert, I need you to hold this for me.' He passed him the sword.

Bert took the weapon stupidly and looked around at his classmates. They still appeared terrified, but they had stopped running around at least. Instead, they were all staring at the Professor. Bert was still a little dazed from what had happened with the mirror, but he began to piece his thoughts together. 'Those machines coming to life,' he said. 'Was that magic?'

The Professor smiled. 'It certainly was,' he said. He reached inside the case where the armour stood and began to study the metalwork with his fingers. 'Although I have to admit I wasn't expecting quite such a dramatic display. They surely wouldn't have put those things in an open basement if they thought they were fully active. What *did* you do to that mirror?'

'Nothing,' said Bert. 'I just looked in it, and I sort of drifted away. I saw something. I was at the royal palace, I think.' He shuddered as the memory came back to him.

The Professor nodded thoughtfully.

'And you're really a pirate?' said Bert.

'I'm afraid I am,' said the Professor. 'Or so they tell me.'

'What are you stealing?'

'Legs,' said the Professor. He wrenched at the hips of the suit of armour as he spoke, and pulled both legs off, sending the whole structure clattering to the ground.

'What do you need those for?' said Bert.

The Professor tapped his nose. 'That would be telling,' he said. 'Now, if you'll excuse me, Bert, I'm afraid my little disguise plan has generated a lot more noise that I intended. I think it's about time I was leaving.' He wrapped up the legs in his cape and tied them behind his back. One of them jolted and kicked him in the ribs. 'Good to see they're still touch-responsive,' he said in a pained voice. 'She'll be pleased, as long as they don't kick me to pieces along the way.'

'Who'll be pleased?' said Bert.

The Professor shook his head. 'It's a long story.'

'Won't the lawmen catch you?' said Bert.

The Professor knelt and lowered his voice. 'About that, Bert,' he said. 'There might be some people asking you questions about what happened here – dangerous people. It's important that you don't get yourself into trouble. Don't say anything that might suggest you had anything to do with the magic here. And don't mention anything about that mark, all right?'

'Why would they think I had anything to do with it?' said Bert.

The Professor studied him for a moment. 'Best to be careful,' he said. There was a shout from upstairs, and the rending crack of a door being forced open.

The Professor took the sword from Bert's grasp. 'Farewell,' he said.

There was a rush of footsteps, and two blue-coated figures burst into the room. 'No one move,' they shouted, as they drew their swords. 'Back against the wall.'

The Professor was already rushing to meet them. He delivered a strong kick to the closest man before he could defend himself and sent him flying into the wall.

'Criminal scum!' yelled the next man, swinging his weapon. Bert saw a flash of movement and heard a clang as the blades met. There was a whistle of sharp metal.

The man in blue leapt back and raised his weapon in a block but the Professor was faster – forcing him back, moving his blade around his opponent's guard.

'Surrender,' yelled the guard.

There was another sharp clang, and the thud of a heavy punch, and the blue-coated man fell back on the floor, clutching his side. By the time Bert looked up from where the man had fallen, the Professor was already through the exit.

Chapter 3

B ert sat alone in the school office, clenching his bandaged palm and trying not to appear nervous. He had been expecting punishment at school, but this was different. Mr Fitzroy had been furious, of course, and given him detention for a month. But now he sensed that he was in real trouble – deeper trouble than he had ever known. There was a knock at the door.

The handle turned. A man entered.

'Don't get up,' said the man. He was reading a file as he spoke. He pulled out a chair across from Bert and sat down. He was younger than Bert had expected, but he had a heavy aura of authority. He wore a long coat like a soldier, but with a short-peaked cap instead of a helmet or the tall hats that officers usually wore. He carried two swords in his belt, and there was a scar down the right side of his face that his beard didn't quite hide. 'My name is Cassius,' said the man. 'I'm a quæstor. I'm here to ask you a few questions. Is there going to be a problem with that?' He rested his hands on his sword hilts as if he expected Bert to attack.

Bert swallowed and shook his head. *I'm done for,* he thought. He'd never heard of anyone at school being interviewed like this before, but he had heard of the quæstors. They were a secretive branch of the government. People said they only came after the very worst criminals.

'What's your name?' said Cassius.

'Bert.'

'How old are you?'

'Thirteen.'

'Ah,' said Cassius. He smiled coldly. 'Well, I've heard about the museum from other people, Bert. But I'm curious to hear what you have to say about it.' He paused. 'Go on.'

Bert wasn't sure how to reply. But he was certain that he shouldn't tell the truth. It was one thing for people like Freston to joke about 'going magic', but it was quite another to claim that he had experienced it in real life.

They would think he was mad. Or worse, they might believe him. Bert sensed that somehow that would get him into even more serious trouble.

'I don't know what happened,' said Bert. 'I think I knocked my head when everyone was shouting and running around. And I cut my hand on something too. There was a lot of broken glass around.' He pulled the bandage tighter. The burn still tingled strangely. He had managed to keep it hidden from everyone so far. 'When I woke up the Professor was there. He told me to hold a sword for him while he stole some things. Then he just, you know, ran away.'

'After striking two royal guards?' said Cassius.

'Yes, after that,' said Bert. 'That was very bad of him.'

Cassius nodded. He seemed almost amused. 'Well put,' he said. 'It seems you often get into trouble at school. Can you explain that to me?'

Bert was more prepared for this. 'I suppose I get distracted sometimes.'

'Distracted how?'

'I just don't focus on my work. I find it boring or too difficult. I think I'm not as clever as the other children. They pick on me for it.'

Cassius nodded. 'I have some test results that suggest you're actually much cleverer than most of your class-mates. Can you explain that?'

'Those must be old tests.'

'Why?'

'I used to try harder.'

'So you don't apply yourself any more?'

'No,' said Bert. 'Not really. Maybe I'll try harder in future.' He looked down at the floor and clenched his fists. Lying didn't come easily to him.

'Does your father pay for your schooling?' said Cassius.

'No, sir,' said Bert. 'They tell me my father went away to sea and didn't come back, after my mother died. I live here now, and I get money from a scholarship . . .'

Cassius interrupted. 'Do you remember your parents?'

Bert hesitated. 'No,' he said. 'At least, I think I remember them sometimes, but only in dreams. I was ill when I was very small – just before I joined the school – and they say I lost my memories then. It's like there's this fog where everything should be.'

Cassius cleared his throat and looked at the file, considering something. 'Had you ever met Professor Roberts before the museum?' he said.

'No.'

'Has he ever written a letter to you, sent a messenger?'

'No, sir.'

'Do you know what Professor Roberts does?'

Bert was confused. 'Well, I think he's a pirate.'

'Do you know what that means, Bert?'

'I'm not sure,' said Bert. He felt relieved not to have to talk about himself for a moment, but something about the quæstor's tone told him he was still being tested. 'I mean, everyone knows that he steals things,' he said. 'I suppose he makes money from treasure that he finds in Ferenor, when he's exploring the ruins, you know, without proper permission.'

Cassius gave a short laugh. 'That's one way of putting it,' he said. 'Listen, Bert – we need to talk about something serious. Have you heard the story of the metal mage?'

'No,' said Bert. He shuddered. After all that had happened, magic seemed like a risky subject to discuss with anyone – let alone with a quæstor.

Cassius leant closer. 'It's an old story but it's a good one. There's this mage who can turn things to metal. This mage has weak hands. So, what he does is he makes himself metal hands. Then he thinks: *Now my hands are strong but my feet are weak, so I'd better make myself metal feet.* And he keeps going on like that until his whole body is metal. Only his brain is left. *Ah*, he thinks, *Now my body is strong but my mind is weak. I need to make myself a metal mind.* So he does. Only with a metal mind you can't be the same person any more. Do you know what happens next?'

'No, sir,'

'The mage kills everyone he used to love, all his friends and family, and no one can stop him. All because he made himself a pair of metal hands.'

There was a pause in the interview. Bert didn't know what to say. He felt a growing dread in his stomach, worse than any time he'd been disciplined by the teachers or told lies to his friends. *Any moment,* he thought. *Any moment now he'll draw his swords.* He wondered if it would help to confess to the quæstor first: to tell him about the mark on his hand. But somehow he knew it wouldn't save him. It was too late now for anything except silence.

The quæstor clapped his hands suddenly.

Bert flinched in his seat.

'Magic isn't like a fairy story,' said Cassius. 'It's a very dangerous thing. Have you ever wondered why there isn't a Kingdom of Ferenor any more?'

Bert felt uneasy. 'Magic never existed,' he said. 'It's a myth.'

Cassius waved his hand dismissively. 'But suppose the stories were true – suppose there was magic in the world. Do you think that would be a safe thing?'

Bert felt confused. 'But even if they were true, there aren't any mages any more, are there?' he said. 'I mean, even in the myths, they died when Ferenor fell to ruin.'

He tried to keep his voice steady, but he had the uneasy feeling the quæstor could see through his bluff. In fact, Cassius almost seemed amused.

'Even still, we must be prepared,' he said. 'Do you understand?

'I think so.'

Cassius stared at him sternly and lowered his voice. 'I have to be certain you understand, Bert, because the old laws of Penvellyn decree that when a person is proved to have engaged in magic practices, they don't get second chances. And neither do the people that protect them.'

Bert blinked. 'You're letting me . . .?' he blurted out before he could stop himself. He covered his mouth and looked down. *Keep quiet,* he thought. *It's a trick. He just wants you to admit you had something to do with the accident at the museum before he takes you away to prison.*

Just then there was another knock at the door. A man wearing a light grey suit entered the room. Bert felt a jolt of horror as he recognized the man's face. It was Prince Voss: the man he had seen through the mirror. The prince appraised him with cold eyes, and gave a brief smile.

'Quæstor,' he said.

'Prince Voss,' said Cassius. He stood up and gave a short bow. 'I wasn't expecting you to come here yourself, sir. There's really no need for your presence.'

'Isn't there?' said Voss. He strode across the room and stood behind Bert's chair with his hand on his sword hilt. Cassius's expression became stern and unhappy, as if he was about to do something unpleasant. All at once Bert felt the chill of impending death.

Cassius remained standing as he faced the other man. 'Your Highness,' he said. 'This is government business, and I'm afraid I must insist that you leave.'

Voss made no move to go. 'I hear a lot about government business these days,' he said. 'It used to be that the word of the royal family was reason enough for anything.' He gripped the back of Bert's chair until it made a creaking sound. 'You should be more open to conversation, quæstor,' he said. 'After all, I hear you are going to be spending time under my command very soon.'

Cassius gave a slight start. 'It's true that the inquiry requires me to spend time on your airship, sir. However, I remain under the command of the government.'

Voss snorted. 'I tend to find things work better if the men on my ship follow my orders. Ferenor is a dangerous place. Terrible things can happen to the unprepared.'

'I will be sure to be careful,' said Cassius, coldly.

Bert didn't fully understand what was happening between the two men, but it was obvious that he had stumbled into some long-standing argument between the government and the royals. The men stared at one another for a moment before Bert sensed Voss's grip loosen from his chair.

'I felt I should be here in person,' said Voss. 'After all, it was my father that opened the exhibit at the museum. I feel somehow . . . responsible, for what happened.'

Bert felt a shudder as he remembered the sensation of being pulled through the mirror, and finding the prince waiting on the other side. He tried to remain calm.

'I'm sure no one would suggest such a thing,' said Cassius.

'This is the boy who had the . . . accident?' said Voss.

'We were just discussing the details,' said Cassius. He glanced at Bert. 'It seems he had a nervous episode, due to the noise and the lights. He fainted.'

'Poor boy,' said Voss. His voice remained cold. 'It must have been quite the ordeal, meeting that crazed pirate on the loose. Especially in such an odd place.'

'Indeed,' said Cassius. 'Anyway, I had just finished here.'

Bert held his breath and waited.

'And?' said the prince, taking a step forwards. There was a slight scrape of metal as he adjusted his grip on his sword.

'And everything's fine, Prince Voss,' said Cassius, with a note of insistence. 'We just had a talk. There's no problem. In fact, Bert's just leaving, aren't you, Bert?'

Bert's breath returned to him. 'Yes, sir,' he said. He took a last look at Cassius – the lawman was trying to get him out of the room. He didn't need to be told twice; he gave a swift bow and headed towards the exit.

Voss stepped forwards and put his hand on Bert's shoulder. The grip felt cold and unnaturally heavy. His fingers were as hard as metal.

Bert froze.

'I can tell you something interesting,' said Prince Voss. 'Magic is of course a joke to children these days. We've moved on in the world. Become more enlightened. But if someone was suspected of being a mage in the old days of Penvellyn, do you know what happened, boy?'

Bert didn't look at the prince. He shook his head.

Voss leant closer. 'They were immediately put to death,' he said.

Cassius cleared his throat. 'An interesting history lesson,' he said. 'But I'm afraid the boy really should leave now. I'm sure he's being missed by his school friends.'

'Very well,' said Voss. He released his grip, and Bert hurried from the room.

Thankfully no one followed him into the corridor.

There were no schoolmates upstairs in his dormitory when he entered. Everyone was still in classes. He went to the window and looked out, waiting for the nausea to pass. The grey buildings of Penvellyn City glowed in the sunset, horses and carriages swept by on the wide roads, and everything looked calm and orderly. But inside Bert knew something had changed. He felt as if he'd seen the underneath of his world for a moment. It would never seem peaceful again.

Chapter 4

Two days after he met Prince Voss, Bert was still having bad dreams. There had been a shadow in his latest one – people crying out in the streets – a fire. He dreamt he was looking into the mirror again, only this time a strange face was staring back at him. The face suddenly called his name.

He sat up in bed and let out a long breath. Then he looked under the bandages on his palm. The burn hadn't healed at all. In fact, it seemed to be getting worse. He'd been feeling strange too. Sometimes he thought he saw things out of the corner of his eye.

A ball of paper bounced off his head and landed on the bedsheets.

'Hey, Bert,' yelled Freston. 'Hope you're ready to lose.'

'What?' said Bert.

'Open it,' said Freston.

Bert looked at the notice on the paper – apparently, the yearly sword fighting exams were being held today. There was also a crudely drawn picture of him with 'loser' written above. He frowned at Freston. 'How long were you waiting for me to wake up?'

'You're going to lose,' said Freston.

After everything that had happened, it was hard to believe that all the aspects of school life – the bullying and the squabbling and the silly jokes told around the fireplace – were continuing as usual. 'Yeah, I got that part,' said Bert. 'Was there anything else?'

Freston flushed. For a moment, he seemed to struggle for a response. 'I should have known you'd have no pride,' he said. He clenched his fists and stormed out of the dormitory.

Bert chuckled to himself. But as he looked around he realized everyone was already down at breakfast. He'd be lucky if there was anything left to eat.

He dressed hurriedly and slid down the bannister of the spiral staircase, avoiding Freston's cronies along the hall. Ever since the events in the museum – which all the children now agreed were a simple accident, some kind of malfunctioning display – Bert had faced a lot of hostility.

People seemed to blame him for helping the Professor. It made school even more uncomfortable than usual. As he weaved through the canteen, trying to find anything edible amongst the service trays, he noticed an unfamiliar girl sitting across the room. She had pale hair and a serious face, and she seemed to be watching him over her bowl of porridge.

He sat down beside Norton – a permanently depressed-looking boy who was the only real friend he felt he could trust – and began to eat his dry toast. Norton hadn't been at the museum, and didn't seem especially interested in what had happened either. He never seemed especially interested in anything, except dismal poetry. 'Who is that?' said Bert, nodding at the girl.

'Oh, her,' said Norton. 'She's new.'

'When did she turn up?'

'They introduced her while you were with . . . you know,' said Norton. He didn't seem to want to talk about the quæstor either. 'You like your toast dry?'

Bert ignored the question. 'Where's she from?'

'No one knows,' said Norton. 'She hasn't spoken to anyone since they introduced her. I expect she's perfectly miserable. I can't say I blame her, really.'

Bert tried to concentrate on chewing his breakfast, but every time he looked up the girl was still watching him. She didn't seem to care when he tried staring back.

'Good breakfast?' said Norton.

'Not really,' said Bert between mouthfuls. 'Better than nothing.'

Norton sighed. 'That's the spirit.'

The girl was still staring at Bert as he rose to put his plate away. He avoided her table and passed a group of girls gathered around the morning newspaper. They seemed to be excited about something on the front page and didn't pause to give Bert their usual cold stare.

'I heard it was a man dressed in black,' said Garnet.

'I heard it wasn't a person at all,' said Samantha. She lowered her voice. 'It was a ghost. It ran straight through the front doors and started destroying the place.'

'That's stupid,' said Garnet. 'There's no such thing.'

Olivia shook her head. 'They could see the flames from Portside.'

Bert felt a chill. He hesitated for a moment, then dropped his plate into the wash rack and approached their table. 'What are you talking about?' he said.

'There was a fire at the museum,' said Garnet. 'Someone destroyed the special collections wing. They say if it had spread it could have burnt down half the city.'

'That place obviously wasn't safe,' said Samantha. 'I mean, after the accident *your friend* caused, I suppose we're lucky to have got off with a few lights and noises.'

Bert tried not to show any reaction to the news, but as

he made his way back upstairs he felt troubled. He had a vague impression that the museum had been in his dreams, along with a fire in the sky and people shouting. But with so much on his mind, it was hard to say for certain.

'What you learn here could save your life,' bellowed Mr Pavlo, as Bert's class gathered on the duelling field. The grass was still wet with dew, and people were watching from the grey windows of the school building. 'You all know the rules by now,' said the fighting instructor. 'It will be an elimination contest until we get to the final five. You may only be using stick-swords today, rather than cold steel, but I still expect you to fight like you mean it.'

Bert looked across at his first opponent. Norton was chewing on a grass stalk and holding his stick loosely over his right shoulder. 'Are you ready?' said Bert.

Norton made a non-committal gesture.

'Keep your guard up, everyone,' yelled Mr Pavlo. 'You're meant to be simulating what you would do in a real fight, not preparing for a dance.'

'This *is* what I'd do in a real fight,' mumbled Norton. Without waiting for the signal, he stepped forwards lazily and swung his stick over Bert's head.

Bert dodged and tapped him with a swift strike.

'And so I die,' said Norton. He gave a brief bow. 'Good luck, Bert.' He knocked aside the daisies with his stick as he walked away to the observation benches.

'What are you doing over there?' asked Mr Pavlo.

Bert looked around. 'I just finished my first fight—'

'No dawdling,' interrupted Mr Pavlo. 'Come over here and get ready. I shall expect you all to strike at each other with full swings. Don't forget to use grapples too.'

Bert was used to teachers not listening to him. He caught the new girl staring at him again. She was close enough to speak to this time. 'Can I help you?' he said.

She grinned, and twirled her practice sword.

Bert was beginning to feel uneasy about her.

'All right, Bert,' said Mr Pavlo. 'You're against Freston.'

Bert sighed inwardly. He badly wanted to beat Freston, but his opponent had been exam champion every year. He wished sometimes that he could stop caring, like Norton. As he looked over he saw that his friend was picking flowers rather than watching the contest.

'I'm surprised you even got this far,' taunted Freston. 'I hope you have a defence for the Hyperion gambit.' He swished his stick over his head. 'If you even know what that is?'

Bert ignored him and raised his stick over his right

shoulder, waiting for Mr Pavlo to give the signal to commence. He was determined not to let Freston get to him.

Freston grinned as they waited. 'You look pathetic.'

Bert kept his gaze steady, trying not to show any reaction.

'I'm not even going to feel proud of beating you.'

Bert remained silent.

'Did your parents abandon you out of shame?'

Bert felt a flash of anger. His hands shook.

'Go,' yelled Mr Pavlo.

Bert leant on to his back foot as Freston stepped in, then lunged forwards. He aimed straight for his opponent's head, putting his full power behind the blow.

Freston brought his stick up to block the attack.

There was a sharp crack.

Two halves of stick went spinning through the air and Freston collapsed on the grass, clutching his arm and gasping in pain. 'That's not fair,' he whined. 'He cheated.'

Bert felt elated for a moment, but he quickly realized that something was wrong. As he looked down he saw a faint red glow pulsing from behind his bandages. *Not now*, he thought. He glanced worriedly at the classmates nearby, wondering if anyone had noticed.

'What's going on over here?' said Mr Pavlo.

Bert clenched his fist. 'Nothing,' he said. His panic grew as he thought of having to face the quæstors again.

A stinging sensation spread up his arm.

'He must have put metal in his stick,' said Freston. He stood up and retrieved the broken halves of his weapon. 'Nothing could have broken through my practice sword.'

Mr Pavlo took both sticks and stared at them for a moment. 'I see what you mean, Freston,' he said. 'You've clearly been doctoring your stick with filcher's putty, haven't you – making it as hard as a rock?' His face darkened. 'So not only have you cheated in my exam, and lost, but you also have the nerve to accuse this other boy, whose weapon is perfectly normal.'

Freston turned pale. 'But he snapped it in two.'

'You will see me later,' said Mr Pavlo. 'Perhaps this explains how such a talentless sprig could win so often.' He cleared his throat. 'Something wrong with your hand?'

'No, sir,' said Bert hurriedly.

'All right,' said Mr Pavlo. 'You progress to the next round.'

Bert would have liked to enjoy his victory over Freston, but he was too afraid of what was happening to him. He stood in line with the remaining competitors and dared a peek under the bandages. The mark was still there, but to his relief it seemed to be fading.

'Does it hurt?' said the new girl.

Bert flinched. She had been standing behind him the

whole time. She must have seen the mark. He froze for a moment, unsure of what to say.

The girl seemed to be smiling at him.

'Listen up,' said Mr Pavlo. 'The first play-off will be Bert, against . . . sorry, what's your name?'

'Finch,' said the girl, in a strong, clear voice.

'Finch against Bert,' said Mr Pavlo. 'You two seem to be our best fighters this year. I look forward to seeing what you will make of one another.'

Bert was too shocked to say anything as the girl led him over to the central duelling court. She carried her stick casually under her arm. 'Good luck,' she said.

'Yeah, good luck,' managed Bert. He lifted his stick over his shoulder and tried to remain focused. A string of questions ran through his mind about the girl: Did she understand what she'd seen? Would she tell on him? He felt like he was caught in a trap.

The girl suddenly shot towards him.

Bert jolted and swung his sword in a desperate block. He hadn't heard the signal to go. He felt a rattling thud as the sticks connected and leapt back as something whistled by his ear.

The girl seemed to move around him in a blur.

Bert blocked again as a swipe shot towards his stomach and the impact almost threw his weapon out of his hand. 'Woah!' He swung his guard back to centre.

The girl ducked around his block and kicked.

Bert brought his arms down to meet the blow but the force of it hit him like a sledgehammer. He flew backwards and hit the ground with the heavy thump.

As his breath returned he had a vague awareness of wet grass against his ears, and Norton reaching down to help him stand. Finch was already preparing for the next fight, but she nodded to him as she took her stance. 'Sorry,' she mouthed, twirling her stick and walking off.

Bert held his ribs. 'What are her feet made of?'

Norton looked at him pityingly. 'That's why I don't try.'

At least no one was looking at him any more. Bert peeked under the bandage and sighed in relief. The glow appeared to have faded completely, but he hardly felt good about the idea of it starting again at any moment. Something must have triggered it. The more he thought about it, the more certain he felt that it had been his anger. He couldn't afford to let that happen again.

Chapter 5

·······························

Bert was still bruised and sore as he made his way across the school courtyard after classes that evening. He hung back from the rest of his schoolmates and leant against the archway that led to the dormitories. Small birds skimmed the rooftops. He wasn't sure exactly how long he stayed there, but after a while he became aware that Norton had joined him.

'Are you all right?' asked Norton.

Bert shrugged. He didn't really feel like talking.

'Sword fighting isn't everything,' said Norton.

'I suppose.'

'I mean, what's it even useful for?'

'Not getting killed in a sword fight?' said Bert.

Norton looked thoughtful. 'Yeah, but what else?'

Bert laughed, despite himself. 'It's not really the competition that's bothering me,' he said. 'It's more, just, a feeling I have. Like something's not right.'

'Since the museum?' said Norton.

Bert wasn't used to Norton being so observant. He wanted to trust his friend, but he honestly didn't think it would help to talk. It might even get Norton into trouble too.

'Did the pirate you met use a sword?' said Norton.

'He did,' said Bert. 'He didn't hurt anyone with it, though. He just, sort of, knocked them down, and ran away.'

'He sounds . . . curious,' said Norton.

'He was.'.

'Do you think you'll see him again?'

'The Professor?' said Bert. 'He's a pirate, Norton. I doubt it.'

'Shame,' said Norton. He stared towards the sky for a while. His face had taken on its more usual, bored expression. 'Do you want to hear my poem about a pirate?'

Bert winced. He didn't share his friend's love of poetry, and right now he wasn't sure he'd be able to disguise his feelings. 'Maybe not right now.'

'Later?'

'Of course.'

Norton hesitated, looking a little downcast. 'It's probably not that good anyway,' he said. He walked away, and disappeared into the shadows of the nearest doorway.

Bert closed his eyes and leant against the cool stone wall. He wasn't sure if anger was the only strong feeling that might provoke the mark in his hand, or if other things might set it off too. Over the course of the day he'd made an effort to avoid strong emotions.

But he was beginning to wonder how long it could last.

Something caught his eye across the courtyard. There was a figure moving by the high wall that joined the street. As he watched, the figure crouched and sprang upwards.

Bert gasped. Whoever it was had jumped on to the top of the wall – three times their own height – like it was nothing. He blinked and looked again. The person was still there, looking back towards the school. He thought he caught a glimpse of long hair but it was hard to tell in the low sunlight. Then the figure was gone – leaping down the other side of the wall.

He squinted at the wall. 'What on earth was that?'

He told Norton what he'd seen later as they prepared for bed.

'Are you sure it was real?' said Norton.

'Do you think I'd be talking to you if I wasn't?'

'I don't know,' said Norton. 'I don't really know why people talk to me at all.'

Bert lay back on his pillow. Sometimes it was frustrating having a friend who didn't care about these things. 'I just feel like something strange is going on,' he said.

'Well, if I was a different sort of person, I'd say we should sneak out of the school and investigate. We could make some disguises, and try to follow their trail.'

Bert turned to face him. 'Couldn't we be that kind of people?'

'No. I don't think so,' said Norton, yawning. A few moments later he was snoring softly, his breath keeping time with the fluttering curtains over the dormitory window.

Bert lay awake for a while, wondering if Norton was right. He secretly thought that he *was* the kind of person that went on adventures. But he had to admit there was a certain appeal in leaving them aside for the time being. Especially when his bed felt so comfortable.

His dreams were strange and murky. There was some kind of shadow following him. Every time he looked around it was a few paces behind, beckoning to him, as if it wanted to talk. There was something familiar about it, but however hard he tried, he couldn't see it clearly. Then the dream changed. He was back in the basement of the museum. The room was filled with ashes. He saw a metal hand searching through the rubble. The hand closed around a fragment of glass and a harsh voice spoke:

'This is where it happened. It's already here.'

Bert woke to the sound of startled voices. He saw the silhouetted shoulders of six boys from his dormitory gathered in the doorway, peering into the corridor. Norton wasn't amongst them. He heard a voice say something about a fire. 'Norton?' he said.

There was no reply. Norton didn't seem to be in the room.

He rose and joined the others. 'What's going on?'

'There was an intruder in Mr Fitzroy's office,' said a tall boy named Rickard, who was peeking over the heads of everyone else. 'They say he burnt something.'

'An intruder?' Bert thought of the figure he'd seen jumping over the wall. He looked around again for Norton, and spotted him by the window. 'What are you doing over there?' he said. 'There's some kind of commotion downstairs. They said it was a fire.'

Norton yawned. 'I'm too tired for all this.'

'You've had plenty of sleep,' said Bert. He lowered his voice. 'Think about it – I saw that strange person hanging around, and now this. Do you think it's connected?'

Norton shook his head. 'It's probably the usual stuff.'

'Usual how?' said Bert.

Norton didn't bother to reply.

Bert heard a stern voice approaching from the corridor. 'You will all go back to your rooms,' said Mr Fitzroy. 'There is no danger to anyone.' He appeared in the doorway, dressed in a sleeping cap and pyjamas. If they'd dared, the boys might have laughed at him. 'You, Bert, will come with me immediately. We will get to the bottom of this matter.'

Bert tensed. 'Me?'

Mr Fitzroy beckoned him impatiently.

Bert followed him downstairs to the teacher's office and found Freston already waiting. The other boy looked pale and worried. There was a strong smell of burning in the air, despite the open window, and he could see fragments of scorched paper littered across the floor.

'What happened here?' said Bert.

'I will ask the questions,' said Mr Fitzroy. 'Where were you for the past hour?'

'In bed,' said Bert.

'Can anyone verify that?'

'People in my dormitory, I suppose,' said Bert. 'I was sleeping.'

Mr Fitzroy picked up a piece of ashen parchment. 'This is all that's left of your school records. Every note we have on you in this school, all gone up in smoke.'

Bert shook his head in disbelief. 'How?'

'That is exactly what I'd like to know,' said Mr Fitzroy. 'Someone must have come down here, unlocked my door – goodness knows how – and burnt it.' He glared at Bert.

Bert felt confused. 'You don't seriously think it was me?' he said. 'Those are my grades. I mean, they're not perfect, but they're still good grades.'

'Didn't you get an F in dance class?' said Freston.

Bert frowned. 'Is that relevant?'

'Mr Pimple said it was the worst dancing he'd ever seen.'

Mr Fitzroy rubbed his brow in obvious exasperation.

Bert suppressed the urge to knock Freston off his seat. 'My point is, there are plenty of good grades there too. I'm the last person who would want to wreck them.'

Mr Fitzroy swallowed and looked down. He seemed to be considering the logic of the matter. 'Let's leave that for now,' he said. 'I also have a report from Freston.'

Bert looked at the other boy. He seemed shaken.

'I-I was attacked by someone,' stammered Freston.

'Speak up,' said Mr Fitzroy.

Freston wiped his eyes. 'I was standing in my dormitory, looking at the stars, and s-suddenly someone picked me up over their head, and threw me out of the window.'

Bert gave an involuntary snort of laughter.

'It's not funny,' snapped Freston. 'I could have been killed. It's only because my pyjamas caught on the window latch that I was saved. I was nearly murdered.'

'What does this have to do with me?' said Bert.

'You've always hated me,' said Freston. His voice quavered. 'You're always pretending you're cleverer than me. You hurt my arm. You snapped my stick in two.'

'That's enough,' said Mr Fitzroy. 'Explain yourself, Bert.'

Bert felt angry at being tied into such a ridiculous story, but he quickly calmed himself. He couldn't afford another mishap like the duelling field. 'Let's think about this,' he said. 'Are you suggesting *I* lifted *you* – a larger person – over my head, and threw you out of a window?'

Freston paused and sniffed. 'Well . . . if it wasn't you . . .?'

'Did you see the person?' said Mr Fitzroy.

'I didn't see anyone,' said Freston. 'They must have snuck up on me.'

'Did anyone else see an intruder?' asked Mr Fitzroy.

Freston looked glum and shook his head.

Mr Fitzroy covered his face with his hand. 'I've had enough of this nonsense,' he said. 'I want both of you to explain exactly what happened today, from the very beginning.'

*

Bert was exhausted when he left the teacher's office. The worry of the day before, and now this disturbance, had taken more out of him than he'd realized. But it seemed he wouldn't be allowed to go straight back to bed. As he headed for the stairs he found Finch, the new girl, waiting for him in the corridor. 'Great,' he said. 'Are you going to kick me again?'

Finch put her finger to her lips. 'Come here,' she said. She led him to a quiet spot beside the staircase. 'What were they talking to you about?'

Bert frowned. 'Why is that any of your business?'

The girl looked exasperated. 'We have serious matters to discuss, Bert,' she said, lowering her voice to a whisper. 'Has that mark on your hand been getting worse?'

Bert felt a chill. 'What do you mean?'

'There's no point in hiding it from me,' said Finch.

Bert put his hand behind his back. 'I don't know what you're talking about,' he said. He felt deeply suspicious of the girl. The memory of his interrogation with the quæstor and Voss came back to him. 'You've made a mistake. I have to go back to bed.'

'I *need* to talk to you,' pleaded Finch. 'You could be in danger.'

'Who's talking out there?' hissed a voice from upstairs.

Finch winced. 'We need to find somewhere private we can talk,' she said. 'Is there anywhere you know about? I still haven't figured out the layout of this cursed place.'

Bert frowned. He badly wanted to confide in someone. But the more he thought about the night's events, the more suspicious he felt of Finch. This could still be a trick or test. His heart was beating fast. He needed to calm down. 'I'm going to bed,' he said. He hurried away before Finch could protest, and quietly closed the door of the dormitory behind him.

Thankfully everyone was in bed again. Norton was talking in his sleep, saying something about sandwiches with ice cream. Bert didn't want him to wake the others.

'Norton, you're dreaming,' he whispered.

Norton blinked and looked around. 'Sorry,' he said. He appeared to be deep in thought for a while. 'Do you think they'll have sandwiches at lunch tomorrow?'

'Probably,' said Bert. 'We usually do.'

'Right,' said Norton. 'Do you think we'll have ice cream?'

'I don't think so,' said Bert.

Norton sighed. 'Nothing's perfect.'

In moments, he was snoring again.

It's too much of a risk, Bert told himself as he lay awake, watching the approaching dawn. The truth was, he wanted to speak to Finch, or at least hear what she had to say. But he couldn't look at his palm now without imagining a glow piercing through the bandages. He thought of how earnest the girl had seemed when she said that she wanted to help him, and felt a shudder of shame. He hadn't realized avoiding his emotions would make him feel like such a coward.

Chapter 6

T he next day wasn't any easier for Bert. The whole school was talking about the fire and the mysterious attack on Freston. Through the course of the day, someone suggested that it must be linked to the strange figure that damaged the museum, and that, inevitably, led to people suggesting Bert had something to do with it. He tried to keep his head down as he headed towards afternoon engineering class, but he noticed Finch hurrying towards him. 'Excuse me,' he said, weaving ahead of the other children in an attempt to get away. A hand suddenly gripped his arm.

'We need to talk,' said Finch.

'How do you move so fast?' said Bert.

Finch stood in his path and lowered her voice. 'Where should we meet?'

'Nowhere,' said Bert. 'Let me past.'

Finch folded her arms and shook her head.

'Hey look,' said Freston, 'Bert's got a girlfriend.'

Finch's fist shot out in a blur and caught him in the stomach.

'Ow,' gasped Freston. He staggered away.

The corridor cleared around Bert and Finch and the other students headed into class. 'I don't want to do that to you, too,' said Finch. 'Let's just go for a talk.'

'This isn't personal,' whispered Bert. 'You might not understand, but if you really want to help, you'd listen to me. I just need everyone to leave me alone.'

'It's for your own good,' said Finch.

'Is there some problem out here?' said Mrs Huttle, the chemistry teacher. She stood in the doorway, tapping a cane against the wall.

'Sorry, ma'am,' said Bert. 'I'm just heading in.'

Apparently, Finch wasn't giving up. She claimed the desk behind him, and when the time came to form pairs for experiments she took hold of his arm and didn't let go. Some of the other children began to giggle. Bert felt his face turning red.

'This is getting embarrassing,' said Bert.

'Embarrassment will be the least of your worries,'

said Finch.

'All right, children,' said Mrs Huttle. 'We're going to be doing . . .' She trailed off and frowned over at Finch and Bert. 'Are you two holding hands?'

'We're fine,' said Bert.

'That wasn't the question,' said Mrs Huttle.

'We're best friends,' said Finch.

Bert gave an inward sigh. The other children laughed.

'I see,' said Mrs Huttle. She shook her head. 'Well, we're doing a chemiluminescent experiment today. It will involve effervescent oil – an expensive ingredient. Any of you that spill a drop of it will be cleaning this whole lab instead of eating lunch. Is that understood?'

'Yes, ma'am,' chorused the class.

Finch looked wickedly at Bert.

Bert grabbed the bottle of oil.

'What?' said Finch.

'You're not getting it,' said Bert. He held the bottle close.

'I wouldn't dream of it,' said Finch.

'Is everyone paying attention?' said Mrs Huttle.

Bert looked over at the blackboard. As he did so he caught a flash of movement out of the corner of his eye and turned just in time to she Finch throw something.

There was a sharp tink as the glass bottle hit the floor, and a pool of hissing chemicals quickly spread at Bert's feet. Only the bottle neck was still in his grasp.

'You have to be joking,' said Bert.

'Whose fault was that?' yelled Mrs Huttle.

Finch grabbed hold of Bert's hand and raised it along with her own. 'That was our fault, ma'am,' she said. 'Silly mistake.' She didn't bother to disguise the satisfaction in her voice.

'I shall expect this room to be spotless when I return,' said Mrs Huttle when she had finished telling them off at the end of the lesson. 'Start by sweeping the floors, and then move on to mopping.'

She closed the door with a thump and turned the lock.

'Right,' said Finch. 'Now we can talk.'

Bert ignored her and began to sweep.

'You know, effervescent oil isn't even that expensive.'

Bert closed his eyes and took a deep breath. He was determined not to lose his temper. He felt like his palm was already prickling under the bandages.

'All right, I'll get straight to the point,' said Finch. She knelt and started fiddling with her shoes. 'You'll understand in a moment,' she said.

'What are you doing?' said Bert.

'You'll see,' said Finch, pulling at her socks.

Bert wondered if Finch was actually insane. It wasn't a pleasant thought, knowing how good she was at fighting, and that there was a locked door between him and help. 'Listen,' he said. 'I don't know what you used to do at your last school, but this isn't normal.'

'I didn't have a last school.'

'What do you mean?'

'There,' said Finch. She slammed her foot down with a thump. There was something shiny and dense where her skin should have been.

The truth began to dawn on him.

'Are your feet . . . metal?' he said.

'Not just metal feet,' said Finch. 'Metal legs. You ought to recognize them, seeing as you played a part in getting them to me.'

Bert was too stunned to speak. He could see the cogs and pivots moving as Finch took a step towards him: just like the suit of armour at the museum. At the back of his mind he recalled Cassius's story of the metal mage.

'It can't be,' he said. He sat down in the teacher's chair and put his head in his hands. Now he wasn't sure if he was the one losing his mind. 'How could you have them?'

'I lost my real legs in an accident a while ago,' said Finch. 'My name is Finch Roberts, and my home is the airship *Lugalbanda*. You've met my father.'

'Roberts?' said Bert. 'You mean the Professor?'

Finch nodded. 'Let me look at your hand.'

Bert allowed her to undo the bandages.

She didn't look pleased. 'This might be worse than we thought,' she said. 'Listen, Bert. That wasn't any normal kind of accident in the museum. We think it might be a magical curse.'

'A curse? What do you mean?'

Finch sighed. 'I know this will be difficult for you to understand. Basically, magical artefacts can be hard to predict. This one seems to have planted some kind of power inside you. It seems to be unstable, and that means it's very dangerous. That's the best way I can explain.'

'Dangerous how?' said Bert.

'Well, for one thing, it might kill you.'

Bert took a long time getting his head around what she was telling him. He looked at his faint reflection on the glossy, varnished desk. There was no doubt in his mind that she was telling the truth, but that didn't offer much comfort. 'So, you came to tell me I'm going to die?'

Finch bit her lip. 'No,' she said. 'At least, not if I can help it. We feel responsible for all this, my father and me. It was my idea to get those legs – you have no idea how annoying it was, getting around on wooden pegs and crutches – but now that I've got what I wanted, I can't just leave you to suffer. I went to see my father last night, and he's forming a plan.'

Bert remembered the figure jumping over the wall. 'It was you I saw?'

Finch looked pleased, but she quickly grew serious again. 'There's another problem with that mark, besides what it might do to you. You know Prince Voss?'

'I've met him,' said Bert. He felt a chill. 'He was here when the quæstor interviewed me. And I saw him in a vision when I had the accident with the mirror.'

'That's not good,' said Finch. 'He's a madman, Bert. For years, he's been collecting artefacts from Ferenor and hiding them away in his private collections. They say that he's obsessed with magic, and that he hunts down anyone that claims to know about it – even kills them if they won't help him. There are all kinds of rumours about people who've disappeared.'

'How can he get away with that?' asked Bert. 'Surely the government would stop him? The royal family haven't been properly in charge of the country for years.'

'He still has enough power to protect him,' said Finch. 'The government would need to gather evidence to stop him, and everyone's too afraid, or too unwilling, to do that. He has a small army of servants and soldiers that help him with his excursions to Ferenor, and they act as his enforcers and spies around Penvellyn. He has his own airship too – the *Vulture* – state of the art, huge guns and engines. Then there's that prison he practically owns at Grimwater—'

'All right,' Bert interrupted. He was starting to feel

queasy about the danger he was in. He shook his head. 'A few days ago, I thought magic was supposed to be fake.'

'Well, that's what Voss wants,' said Finch. 'He's pushed more than anyone to get that museum made. He wants anything to do with magic, and Ferenor, for himself. The government are happy to go along with his lies if it helps them to make their modern world, and their own achievements, look more impressive. And I honestly don't think they believe there's any real danger from the relics of the old world any more. They won't help you, Bert.'

Bert nodded. Instinctively, he knew she was right.

Finch put her hand on his shoulder. 'If Voss finds out you've got some kind of connection with magic, I think you could be in real danger. He won't stop looking for you. We need to get you out of here as soon as possible. I'll tell my father we have to speed up the plan.'

'But what are we going to do?' said Bert.

'We're going to find how to undo that curse,' said Finch. 'I know it might be a shock, but there's really no way you can stay here. No one in Penvellyn can help you with that kind of injury, and if anyone was to find out about it, well, Voss has murdered people for less.'

Bert felt like he couldn't breathe. The idea of running away from school and becoming an outlaw was too much for him to take in. But he knew he couldn't wait around for Prince Voss to return either. Something about the man filled him with terror.

'Are you all right?' said Finch.

'I'm fine,' said Bert, trying to seem calm. 'I'm sorry I wouldn't listen to you before. I was just afraid of what might happen if . . .' He trailed off and looked at his bandaged hand. 'When you say you'll get me out of here, do you mean I'll be, you know, a pirate?'

Finch shrugged. 'We'll worry about that later.'

Bert's stomach felt hollow, but he didn't want to seem nervous and he couldn't deny a faint thrill at the thought of leaving his school life behind – just like he'd dreamt of when he was younger. 'And are you happy with being an outlaw?' he said. 'I mean, running all the time?'

Finch sighed and picked up the broom. 'There are good and bad days,' she said, as she began to clean the room. 'But it's a lot better than this nonsense. Anyway, Bert, now that you finally know the truth, I need you to keep a low profile. I don't know how long it will take for my dad to figure things out, but if Prince Voss finds out about your condition, well – we won't be going on any adventure, that's for sure. So no magic tricks, and no more fires.'

'I'll do my best,' said Bert, feeling increasingly apprehensive about the idea of going on a real adventure. 'It wasn't actually me that started that fire, though.'

Finch looked thoughtful. 'Well, perhaps that's all the more reason to be careful,' she said. 'Someone here seems to have it in for you. We can't let them blow our cover.'

'Agreed,' said Bert.

At that moment the door rattled and Mrs Hutton re-entered the room. She gave them a suspicious look. 'Well, it looks clean I suppose. You'd better leave, Bert. I'm going to have a talk with our new student here about the correct way to behave in the classroom.'

Bert glanced at Finch. There was more he wanted to ask her, but he knew it would have to wait for another time. He felt a little giddy as he went out into the corridor. Everything about school life seemed suddenly distant and pointless. Except, perhaps, for his only friend.

'Are you still avoiding excitement?' asked Norton as they made their way between classes the following day. It was sunny outside, and the other children were laughing and joking.

'I think I might be ill,' said Bert. It was an effort for him not to keep checking his palm, to see if it had grown worse. He began to worry that the strain must be show-ing. 'Listen, Norton. Do you ever think of getting away from this place? Like, leaving for good?'

Norton looked around, as if only considering their

surroundings for the first time. 'Not really,' he said. 'I suppose I do like it better outside, with the trees and the grass.'

'I'm not talking about outside the school,' said Bert. 'I mean, getting away from this place completely. Going away to distant lands.'

Norton looked troubled. It was an expression that Bert hadn't seen in him before, and he began to regret having said anything. 'I suppose I have,' said Norton.

'Don't you think it would be good?'

Norton shook his head. 'I don't know that it would be any better,' he said. 'I mean, I'd still be me. I expect I'd take my problems with me, wherever I happened to go.'

Bert felt deflated. It wasn't what he'd wanted to hear, but he supposed he should have known better than to ask Norton what he thought. His friend still looked troubled, and his discomfort seemed to grow the more Bert glanced at him. 'Forget I mentioned it,' he said.

As they entered Mr Fitzroy's class Norton still looked downcast and confused, and when they sat down he said: 'Sometimes I don't think anywhere feels like home.'

All at once Bert grew deeply uneasy. Norton's words brought up memories of the way he'd felt when he'd first arrived at the school. The more he thought about it the worse he felt. To make matters worse, Finch hadn't turned up to class. He hadn't seen her all morning. He began to worry that there was something wrong with the plan – or that she'd abandoned him.

Mr Fitzroy rapped on the blackboard. 'Can anyone tell me where we finished last time?'

Garnet raised her hand. 'We were talking about ancient beliefs.'

Norton seemed restless. 'Can I be excused?' he said.

Bert glanced at Mr Fitzroy, expecting some kind of harsh response, but the teacher simply nodded and thanked Garnet. Like many of the teachers, he didn't seem to feel Norton was worth bothering with.

Norton got up hurriedly and headed out.

'What kind of beliefs?' resumed the teacher.

'The story of Lugalbanda,' said Garnet.

Bert felt a shock of recognition at the word. He remembered Finch saying that she lived on an airship called *Lugalbanda*.

'Very good,' said Mr Fitzroy. 'Lugalbanda was a name the people of Ferenor gave to a kind of castle kingdom that was supposed to float over the clouds. It appears in numerous stories from the old times.' He paused. 'What do we now know it to be?'

Freston raised his hand. 'Lightning,' he said. 'Research has shown that Lugalbanda is just an old name for storms, back when people didn't know what caused them.'

'Very good,' said Mr Fitzroy. 'This is just one example of how we can compare old myths to what we know in the modern world, and improve upon their superstitions.'

Bert stopped paying attention. His gaze lingered on the map on the classroom wall. It showed the banana-shaped outline of Penvellyn in red, with Penvellyn City at its northernmost tip. To the south were the icy wastes, to the west were the wild lands beyond government control, over the far east sea the Dalis Kingdoms. To the north was the vast island of Ferenor.

He flinched. Reading the name of the old country hit him like an accusation. He clutched his hand and looked around at his classmates, suddenly feeling alone and vulnerable. His friends had disappeared. His hand was hurting worse than ever. He began to feel dizzy.

At the back of his mind he heard the voice of Prince Voss.

'You're telling me this fire was an accident? This was no accident. The mirror worked. I knew it would work. That boy, he did something to it. He brought it into our world. How else can you explain what the guards saw? A ghost, they said – a creature shrouded in black, firing lightning around the room, burning every magical object to ashes. Destroying my collection. How can you say that was an accident? That boy did something. Maybe he doesn't know what he did, but he did something. I want him brought here, now . . .'

Bert felt a sharp pain and jolted back into reality. He put his hand to his cheek, and realized that he was bleeding. Mr Fitzroy was standing over him, holding a cane.

'He's coming out of the trance,' cried a frightened voice.

Bert blinked. It took him a moment to realize the full implications of what had happened. His hand was glowing through the bandages, burning so strong that his fingers looked like spent matchsticks against the light. The other children looked terrified.

'Stop that this instant,' yelled Mr Fitztroy.

Bert froze in his seat. He'd been found out. He couldn't escape being reported and that would mean Prince Voss would hear, if he wasn't already on his way.

Where was Finch?

Mr Fitzroy raised his cane to strike again.

Bert's hand moved automatically. He grabbed the stick before it struck his face and a burst of energy passed through his palm. The cane disintegrated under his touch.

Mr Fitzroy leapt back as if he'd been stung.

'Stay back,' said Bert. His voice shook with terror.

Mr Fitzroy hesitated, then grabbed Bert's arm and pressed his palm down into the desk. 'Stop this wickedness,' he demanded. There was a crack of splintering wood.

Bert panicked. 'Let go of me,' he said.

The desk split into pieces under his hand.

Mr Fitzroy released him and staggered back, pale and shaken. The rest of the class huddled against the opposite wall, apparently waiting for instructions.

Bert couldn't find a way to calm himself. He remembered Finch's warning about the danger of the mark and looked down in horror at the flickering glow beneath his skin.

'Excuse me,' said a deep voice from nearby.

Bert saw a tall man hovering in the doorway. His first thought was that it was Prince Voss, come to take him away. How had he found out about him so soon?

'There has been a crime here,' bellowed Mr Fitzroy. 'It must be reported.'

'I don't think we should do that,' said the man in the doorway.

'What do you mean?' said the teacher. 'Who are you?'

'I'm just here for my friend Bert,' said the man. He stepped into the room to reveal a familiar, mocking smile. 'I'm sorry I couldn't make an appointment.'

'Professor?' said Mr Fitzroy. He backed away in horror.

'Sorry I kept you waiting, Bert,' said the Professor. He strode forwards with no sign of fear and examined Bert's hand. 'I see it's up to its old tricks again.'

Bert felt a wave of relief. He had been so certain it was his enemy. At the sight of the Professor all his fears seemed to vanish. The pain that had been spreading through his arm grew cooler. The light faded. He could sense that his hand was returning to normal.

'Try taking a few deep breaths,' said the Professor.

Bert did as he was told. 'Thank you,' he managed to reply. 'I think it's stopping.'

'We're not quite in the clear yet,' said the Professor.

There was a scrape of metal from across the room. Mr Fitzroy drew an old poker from a cupboard and held it out threateningly towards the Professor. 'That boy is staying here,' he said. 'He has committed a serious crime, under the old laws, and he will be punished.'

The children seemed transfixed by the pirate.

'I don't have time for this nonsense,' said the Professor. He strode towards the teacher. There was a blur of movement, and the poker went skittering along the floor.

'Let go of me,' said Mr Fitzroy, indignantly.

The Professor pushed the man to the back of the room, forced him inside the stationery cupboard and broke the lock with a swipe of his hand. 'Right,' said the Professor. 'I'm sorry to have disturbed your lessons like this, children. We'll be leaving now.'

Bert hesitated for a moment, and looked around for Norton. It seemed cruel to leave without saying goodbye, even under these circumstances. But his friend still hadn't returned.

'Are you all right?' said the Professor.

'There was someone . . .' began Bert.

'There's no time for goodbyes, I'm afraid,' interrupted the Professor. 'The lawmen could already be on their way. We don't want your journey to end here.'

Bert nodded. Norton would have to understand.

'I'm fine,' said Bert. 'Let's go.'

They ran along the corridor, down a spiral staircase and out through a back entranceway into the street. There was a horse and carriage waiting for them. Finch was sitting in the driver's seat, looking particularly pleased with herself. 'Morning, Bert,' she said.

'How did you know I was in trouble?' said Bert.

'We didn't,' said Finch. 'Why, what happened?'

Bert shook his head in confusion. 'I heard Prince Voss's voice. I think he's coming after me. He thinks I had something to do with the fire at the museum.'

The Professor frowned. 'Get in,' he said. 'I'll explain the plan along the way.'

Chapter 7

....

B ert gazed out of the window of the carriage as they hurried past the grimy, grey houses of the side streets. He couldn't really say what he felt: a strange mingling of doubt and relief. It was the kind of feeling that would only become clear in time. The horse's hooves thundered over the cobbles, and the carriage sped up, making for the heart of the city. 'Where are we going?' said Bert.

'First, I should explain what I've found out,' said the Professor. 'This hand of yours is a lot more trouble than I was expecting. I've quizzed all of my contacts, and it turns out that mirror you looked into wasn't taken from any expedition in the official records.'

'What does that mean?'

'It means it was taken from somewhere very unusual. I suppose I should have expected as much after what happened in the museum – I've found a lot of magical objects that respond to simple touch commands, or the will of the person using them, but for things to come alive like that on their own is unheard of. Something strange is at work.'

Bert shook his head. It still felt strange to talk about magic.

The Professor seemed to read his mind. 'I know this is all odd,' he said. 'But we have to focus on the things we do know. Firstly, that the mirror did something to you. Secondly, that Prince Voss isn't very happy with you, and that usually means something unpleasant.'

Bert nodded. 'We need to get out of here.'

'Right,' said the Professor. 'But first we need to find out as much as we can about that mirror. Now, I think I have a way of doing just that. But it won't be easy.' He bit his thumb for a moment, then hammered on the hatch at the front of the carriage.

The hatch slid open to reveal Finch holding the reins of the horse in one hand and a half-eaten apple core in the other. 'What's the problem?' she said.

'How long until we reach the bank?' asked the Professor.

'Maybe five minutes. Do you have a plan yet?'

The Professor slid the hatch closed without replying. 'Anyway, I was saying about the mirror. It might not be in any official records, but I know where they keep the unofficial ones. The tricky thing will be getting access to them. That's why we're going to the bank.'

'Which bank?' said Bert.

'Hammerton National,' said the Professor.

Bert swallowed. The Hammerton bank was in the centre of the city, right next door to the highest law courts and the main government buildings. 'Is that safe?' he said.

The Professor ducked down suddenly.

Bert was about to ask what the matter was when he caught sight of a group of soldiers on the road ahead. There was a whole platoon of them. They appeared to be climbing into battle wagons – a type of fast, horse-drawn carriage with space for riflemen to stand on top.

It was only after the soldiers were well behind them that the Professor sat up again. 'Don't mind me, Bert,' he said. 'Just keeping a low profile.'

'Why are there so many soldiers around in the streets?'

The Professor smiled unconvincingly. 'Don't worry about that,' he said. 'The military might have some idea that I'm still in the city. It hasn't been easy getting all of this information, Bert. Who would have thought getting a pair of legs would cause so much trouble?'

There was a thump from the front of the carriage.

'Not that I'm complaining of course,' said the Professor. 'And I really am sorry you got caught up in all of this. I promise we'll do our best to make things right.'

Bert felt a sinking feeling in his stomach. He already knew he was a fugitive, in a way, but the sight of the soldiers unnerved him. 'So you're sure this bank has what we need?'

'Certainly,' said the Professor. 'And I'm afraid we can't leave without it.'

Bert frowned. 'But you just said that the soldiers are already looking for you. Aren't they likely to catch you if you walk into a bank and ask for something?'

The Professor laughed heartily. 'I'm not going to ask for it,' he said. 'I'm going to steal it, Bert. In fact, with a bit of luck, you're going to steal it for me.'

Finch brought the carriage to a halt at the front steps of the bank. Crowds of people in smart clothes passed on the broad pavement, and a steady procession of carriages rattled along the roads. In the distance Bert could make out a government airship floating towards the port. The entrance of the bank was flanked by marble columns, and the structure rose to an enormous domed roof.

'You look like such a tourist,' said Finch, as she opened the door.

Bert was too stunned to respond to her taunting. He'd heard a lot about the rich district, but he'd never seen it for himself. The buildings seemed too grand to be real.

'I'll be counting on you, Finch,' said the Professor. 'Keep the carriage on standby for as long as possible. Try not to draw too much attention.'

'I wish I was going in with you,' she said.

The Professor hugged her, and she leapt back on to the carriage.

Bert began to get knots in his stomach. It seemed ridiculous to even dream of stealing from this marble fortress in the heart of the city, especially in broad daylight. There were thick bars on every window. 'What are we actually trying to take from here?' he asked.

'That is a very good question,' said the Professor. 'I have reason to believe that there is a vault here that's used for business relating to Ferenor.'

'Why would they keep it in a bank?'

'Because it's a secret,' said the Professor. 'In fact, it belongs to the royal family, I believe. Probably someone you had the misfortune to meet recently.'

'Prince Voss?'

The Professor nodded.

Bert paused on the steps. 'We're stealing records on

magical artefacts, at the city's main bank, from Prince Voss, with the main government buildings just a few blocks away?'

'Don't shout it all over town, Bert,' said the Professor.

They were greeted at the door by a man in a red coat, who invited them into a large foyer. Bert had never seen such a richly decorated room. The floor was marble, and the ceiling was trimmed with gold borders and elaborate designs. 'Where do we go?' said Bert.

'Let's just loiter by the queue for a moment,' said the Professor.

They stood at the back of the line in front of the cashier desks. There were a lot of people ahead of them. Bert kept looking at his feet to avoid the gazes of the security men.

'I have two plans, Bert,' muttered the Professor. 'But I can't decide.' He held out his hands. 'I need you to pick one for me. Right plan, or left plan.'

'Me?' said Bert. 'You're asking me to choose?'

'Beginners have more luck,' said the Professor. He looked amused.

'Fine,' said Bert. He pointed to the Professor's right hand.

'I see,' said the Professor, frowning. 'Well, we'll have to try it.'

'Wait – can I pick again?'

The Professor shook his head. He passed Bert a small metal sphere and said: 'Get rid of this in the waste paper bin over there. It's weighing me down.'

'What is it?'

'Just some junk I've been carrying.'

Bert hesitated, sensing a trick, but he could see there was no point in arguing. He crossed the polished stone floor to the bin. The only person nearby was a security guard, sitting next to a metal door with a sword at his hip. Bert took the sphere out, wrapped it in a handkerchief, and threw it in with the rubbish. He returned to the Professor. 'What shall I do now?'

The Professor nodded towards the security guard by the metal door. He lowered his voice and said: 'There's about to be a distraction. Stay close.'

'What kind of distraction?' said Bert.

'Well, I'm afraid I'm a bit of a liar. I just told a man in the queue that the bank is going out of business. I'd imagine he'll be eager to get his money out.'

Even as he spoke there was a murmur from the waiting customers. 'If he's getting his money I want all of my money out too,' yelled a high voice. A jumble of protests broke out, and the crowd surged forwards to demand their money from the cashiers.

'How will that help?' said Bert.

'It won't, much. But then there's your distraction.'

'My distraction?' said Bert.

'The smoke bomb you just planted,' said the Professor.

Bert's eyes widened in horror. The waste paper bin across the room ignited with a sudden hiss and spewed a cloud of dense, pungent smoke. The plumes filled the room, and the customers and staff staggered around in panic.

'Now we move – fast,' said the Professor.

Bert ran through the smoke with the Professor. People were coughing and shouting all around them. The Professor grabbed the security guard by the collar and said: 'Why aren't you helping to clear the place? Go find the manager this instant.'

The guard muttered something between coughs, then stumbled back and disappeared into the mass of grey. The metal door was left unguarded.

'Isn't it locked?' said Bert.

The Professor twirled a set of keys around his finger. 'I'm not a great pickpocket, Bert,' he said. 'But you don't have to be when there are so many distractions.' He opened the door and led Bert into a long corridor with glass windows at either side. Beyond the windows rows of clerks were hard at work at their adding machines, oblivious to the chaos outside.

'I didn't think it would be this easy,' said the Professor, laughing. His smile dropped as they came to three metal gates. 'Oh,' he said. 'What's this?'

'Isn't this the right way?' said Bert.

The Professor sighed. 'I think I know what's going on here. Two of the doors are alarmed. It's supposed to trick any opportunists. But which do we choose, Bert?'

'I don't know,' said Bert. He felt exasperated with the Professor. 'Why on earth have you brought us here if you don't know the way?'

'Just have a guess,' said the Professor.

'I'm not guessing again,' said Bert. 'It's too dangerous.'

The Professor looked puzzled, then gave Bert a shove. The push carried him towards the middle gate, but some instinct told him to dive to the left at the last moment. He braced and clattered against the bars, and the gate swung open in his hands.

They waited and listened.

'No alarm,' said the Professor. 'Beginner's luck again, Bert. But I'm afraid you have to do the last part alone. I'm going to try and secure our escape route.'

'You pushed me,' said Bert.

'I was just encouraging you,' said the Professor. He passed Bert a key, a large bag, and a diagram. 'Tell the guard down the hall that the password is *verdigris*, and that you're a messenger boy on an important errand for the government. Say it's urgent. He'll lead you to it himself.'

'Where did you get this key?' said Bert.

'That's another story for another day,' said the Professor. 'Look at the diagram once you're inside the vault and it will show you what files to throw in the bag. I know this is all new to you, Bert, but there's really no other way. Just try to focus and do your best.'

Bert took a deep breath. 'All right,' he said. He tried to hide his shaking hands by putting them in his pockets, but his voice still quavered.

'Oh and one other thing,' said the Professor.

'What is it?'

'Try to enjoy it, Bert. We don't rob banks every day.'

Bert frowned in annoyance, but the Professor had already gone.

He moved as fast as he dared down the long passageway, feeling painfully aware of the sound of his footsteps on the hard, polished floor. As he rounded a bend he found himself face to face with a guard sitting at a metal desk. 'Yes?' said the man.

'I – I need to see a vault,' he stammered. 'The password is *verdigris*.'

'You're here alone?' asked the guard.

'I'm in a hurry,' said Bert. 'Files for the Prince.'

'Does the manager know you're here?'

Bert thought for a moment about the best response. He held out his palm and showed the man the key. 'No,' he said sarcastically. 'I broke in.'

The guard laughed. 'Very funny, young sir, but you can't be too careful. Stranger things have happened in Ferenor, as my father used to say.'

Bert tried to look like this was all routine to him as the guard led him through several more gates, locking each one behind them. Then he opened the vault.

'I'll be waiting for you here, sir,' he said.

'Thank you,' said Bert. He stepped inside the dark space, and the door closed behind him with an ominous clang. It took a moment for the amphor lights to ignite.

The room was almost circular, and much bigger than he'd expected. Tall paintings of strange landscapes hung along the curved walls, while a ring of shelves nearby held all kinds of curiosities – from simple vases to the kind of complex machines he'd seen in the museum. He noticed one row that held various metal hands, some of which were tipped with edged weapons. Another cabinet was filled with strange glowing orbs that seemed to give off heat. There were books and notes everywhere too, and a whole quarter of the wall covered in maps of Ferenor.

His gaze was drawn to a long shelf arrayed with a collection of large lanterns, like the ones he'd seen at the museum. There were countless diagrams alongside them with revisions and notes – something about using crystals to cast the right sort of light. One diagram showed an airship directing a large lantern towards a cloud; another showed a picture of a large castle.

He couldn't make any sense of them.

He noticed a desk with a pen and an uncovered ink-stand in the centre of the room, and realized with a stab of panic that someone might have been using the vault recently. The thought that Prince Voss himself might walk in at any moment brought his fears to life.

He hurriedly began to follow the Professor's instructions, counting his paces until he came to a set of filing drawers. Inside were rows of dated entries, some of which had the names of airships printed across the top, others with long series of numbers. He tossed all of them into the bag and took a few deep breaths, reassuring himself that this was the right thing to do. He had never stolen anything before. Diving straight into capital crime wasn't easy for him.

As he made his way back towards the door he noticed a large painting on the wall. It showed a green landscape, and far above it a large castle floating in the clouds.

He was struck by the detailing of the picture.

There was a note beside it, with pictures of various airships and the names of their captains. Some of the names Bert vaguely recognized. There were crosses through all of them except one: Professor Roberts. It made Bert feel uneasy, but it also reminded him that the

Professor was waiting. He moved on quickly, lugging his heavy bag over his shoulder.

Just then he heard the vault door open.

Bert flinched, and looked up.

Three security guards were waiting for him at the doorway. One of them was holding the remains of the metal sphere that had started the paper bin fire.

'Come with us, please, sir,' said the guard who'd let him into the vault. 'There are some people out here that have some questions for you.' He took the bag from Bert's grasp. 'I think they'll be interested to see what you were trying to take from our vaults, won't they?'

Bert's heart sank. He put his hands in his pockets and allowed himself to be marched back to the foyer. The customers had vanished and the Professor was handcuffed to the front desk. He had a bruise on his face and his sword was gone. Around him stood a dozen men wearing long coats and short-peaked caps. Bert felt a chill in his bones. The men were clearly quæstors. Cassius stood at the centre of the group, looking dangerously angry.

'Hello, Bert,' said Cassius. 'I hoped I wouldn't see you so soon.'

Chapter 8

....

Bert was pushed forwards by the security guards. He staggered and came to rest beside the Professor at the long front desk. 'Sorry,' he said. The guards began to handcuff him.

'Don't worry about it,' said the Professor.

Cassius gestured to the guards to stop. 'There's no need to shove the boy around,' he said. 'In fact, you gentlemen can leave now. We have the situation in hand.'

The lead bank guard looked confused. 'Are you sure that's safe, sir? He was using some strange tricks. Wouldn't it be better if . . .?'

'We're quite safe,' said Cassius, curtly.

The guards looked nervously at one another and left the room.

Cassius lowered his voice so that only Bert could hear him. 'This was not a smart choice, after the warning I gave you.' He rested his hand on the hilt of his sword.

Bert was too nervous to think of a reply. The Professor cleared his throat and gave him a reassuring look, but it was clear that he was in no position to help.

'You need to talk to us, Bert,' said Cassius. 'I know when I spoke to you before I didn't press you on what happened at the museum. But there's no choice now. Things are developing quickly and I need to know where we stand if I'm going to be able to protect you.'

Bert bit his lip. He couldn't meet the quæstor's gaze.

'What really happened with the mirror?'

Bert glanced at the Professor.

'What do you mean "protect" him?' said the Professor. 'You government types are all the same. You talk about justice, but you're as crooked as the royals ever were.'

'Don't listen to him,' said Cassius. 'Look at me. We want to help. But you have to start by telling us the truth. What exactly happened to you in that museum?'

Bert looked at the faces of the assembled quæstors. They each looked equally grave and intent, with their hands hovering close to their swords.

'Bert, if you don't talk now, you'll regret it,' said Cassius.

'You know, quæstors used to kill people that used magic,' said the Professor. He gave Bert a significant nod. 'I wouldn't be inclined to trust anyone with a history like that.'

The hint wasn't lost on Bert.

'That was hundreds of years ago,' said Cassius, angrily. 'And I will not take lectures on honesty from a pirate. You have no idea what you're meddling with, Roberts.'

Bert felt thoroughly confused. He rested his back against the desk, and considered his situation. He didn't trust Cassius, but he didn't see a way out.

'I'll be direct,' said Cassius. 'Something bad is going on in this country. I want to stop it, before it gets out of hand. We believe that you can help.'

The Professor snorted and shook his head. 'Don't listen to him, Bert.'

Bert swallowed and glanced at his hand.

'Are you all right, Bert?' said Cassius.

Bert nodded. He didn't understand why the quæstor was pretending to be nice to him. Given the situation, it was more unnerving than being treated like a criminal. He began to wonder if all of this was some elaborate trick – maybe Voss and the quæstors were in it together.

The more frightened he became the stranger he felt. It

wasn't just nerves. There was a cold sensation spreading over his hand, getting worse with each passing moment.

Cassius's eyes narrowed suspiciously. 'What have you got there?'

'Nothing,' said Bert. He backed away.

Cassius grabbed hold of Bert's arms and pulled at the bandage. The cloth gave way, and the red light shone across the room. The quæstors behind Cassius took a step back.

You need to get away, said a quiet, eerie voice.

Bert felt a chill. It was clear that no one else had heard the voice. Someone, or something, was speaking directly to his thoughts, just like back at the museum.

'Let go of him,' demanded the Professor, struggling against his handcuffs.

'What is this mark?' said Cassius. 'Tell me.'

On instinct Bert opened his palm. A shockwave burst out from his hand with a noise like a cannon. It blasted Cassius and the quæstors away and sent them skidding along the floor. The Professor ducked away from the blast. He struck his fists down hard on the floor, and smashed the lock off the handcuffs. When he stood straight again he was free from his restraints.

Bert blinked in astonishment and looked at his hand. The light fluttered and extinguished, like an amphor lamp, and the scar on his palm returned to normal. 'Did

I do that?' he said.

The Professor let out a long breath. 'You'd know better than me, Bert,' he said. He picked up his sword and the bag of files they'd stolen and gestured for Bert to follow. 'Perhaps this isn't the time to worry about it.' As he spoke an alarm bell started ringing and the security gates began to close.

Two of the quæstors found their feet and tried to intercept them.

The Professor blocked their swords with a deft swipe of his blade and swung a pair of punches that knocked them down unconscious. 'Keep up, Bert,' he yelled.

Bert was running as fast as he could. The iron gates had almost descended over the main exit. The Professor ducked and rolled underneath, barely squeezing through.

Bert looked at the gap and hesitated. 'I can't,' he said.

'Stop right there!' shouted Cassius from across the room.

The Professor's arms suddenly appeared under the door, grabbed Bert by the ankles and pulled him down through the opening. He felt the metal scrape against his ribs.

He emerged on the other side as the door closed with a sharp clang. The bank alarm grew muffled behind him. 'You almost got me crushed,' he said.

The Professor didn't seem to hear him. 'That should

keep them busy for a minute,' he said, cheerfully. He helped Bert up and ran out into the open. A group of soldiers were approaching in a horse-drawn battle wagon. 'Where's Finch got to?' he muttered.

A carriage shot out from an alleyway down the street. Finch was at the reins. She kept her head down and urged the horse on as musket shots whistled by. 'I don't have time to stop!' she yelled, her voice somehow carrying over the rumbling of the wheels and the panic in the street.

'Jump for it, Bert,' said the Professor.

'*What?*' gasped Bert. He stared at the approaching hooves.

The Professor gave him another push.

Bert hit the side of the carriage with a thump and clung on. A strong grip helped him up, and in another moment he was inside the compartment with the Professor. Behind him the sound of gunfire grew distant. The buildings of the central district passed in a blur.

A few minutes later the hatch at the front of the carriage slid open.

'We're clear for now,' said Finch. 'I've got an idea, Dad.'

Bert's hands were shaking. 'Why aren't you watching the road?' he said.

Finch frowned. 'I can do two things at once.'

'What's the idea, Finch?' said the Professor.

Finch spat out an apple seed. 'Steam train,' she said.

The Professor took out a pocket watch, considered it for a moment and nodded. 'We've already missed the station. Better aim for the bridge.

The carriage raced through a series of tight bends. Bert could smell burning wood and gum from the spinning wheels. He still felt shocked about what had happened in the bank, but there was no time to worry about it now. Finch opened the window hatch again. 'Just a little further,' she yelled. She uncorked a bottle with her teeth and poured water on to the smoking wheelbase.

'We have one minute to catch the train, by my calculation,' said the Professor.

'Actually, it's about thirty seconds,' said Finch.

'How do you guess that?'

Finch pointed over her shoulder to a plume of steam that had just risen over the rooftops. A shrill whistle sounded. The deep chugging of an engine raced closer. 'Hold on,' she said. The girders of the road bridge loomed into view at the next bend.

'Professor,' said Bert. 'Do you know Cassius?'

'What?'

'It sounded like you knew him.'

The Professor shrugged. 'I worked for the government a long time ago, Bert. Any legitimate explorer has to, if they want to avoid trouble. But I never agreed with their views on magic.' He leant closer to the hatch. 'Finch, I need you to make your own way to the airship rookery. Ditch this carriage and take a cab. The quæstors aren't looking for you yet, so you should be fine.'

'All right,' she said. 'But won't you get there first?'

She brought the carriage to a halt on the bridge. Bert could see the train on the track below. The steam cloud had almost reached them. 'How do we get on board?' he said.

'Just take care of yourself, Finch,' said the Professor.

'You too, Dad,' she said with a smile. They clasped hands before the Professor jumped down from the carriage. He waved for Bert to follow him and strode to the edge of the bridge.

Bert ran to keep up. 'What are we doing here?'

'Catching a train,' said the Professor. Without warning, he grabbed Bert with both arms, and swung him over the top of the railings.

Bert felt a lurch as he dropped, and saw a blur of steam. He landed with a thump against a tarpaulin cover and lay there stunned for a moment.

The Professor landed with a heavy thud a few paces behind him.

'Good luck,' called Finch. She waved to them from the bridge.

The Professor reached down and pulled Bert out of the tarpaulin. They seemed to have landed on the covering of a pile of suitcases. 'Anything broken?' said the Professor.

'No,' said Bert. He found it hard to keep down his annoyance at being thrown around again. He liked to think he might have jumped willingly. 'Just a bit bruised.'

'Good lad,' said the Professor. He patted him hard on the back. 'Now we'd better slip into one of these carriages before we reach the Gulch.'

'What happens then?' said Bert.

'Have you never been out of school?' said the Professor. 'The train locks on to cables and gets a lift across the canyon. It's quite an interesting mechanism, actually.'

'Right,' muttered Bert. He wasn't really in the mood for sightseeing.

'You should go on ahead,' continued the Professor. 'You can scout out the carriage for me, while I fix a disguise for myself. I'll pretend I'm a crazy old man or something.'

What do you mean, pretend? thought Bert, as he rubbed his aching shoulders. He clambered over the luggage and reached the carriage. 'What do I say to the people inside?' he asked. 'Won't they think it's strange that I've just appeared?'

'Tell them you were getting some fresh air,' said the Professor. 'It's all right, Bert. It'll just be market traders and nannies at this time of day.'

Bert nodded, and went to open the door. The hinges were stiff, and when he finally forced it open he stumbled head-first into the compartment.

'Sorry about that,' he called out to no one in particular. Then he glanced up and saw a pair of military boots in front of him. His mouth went dry.

'Are you lost?' said a suspicious voice.

Bert looked around. The carriage was full of soldiers. They wore the light-blue uniforms of Voss's royal guards – like the men Bert had seen at the museum. The person who'd addressed him was a stern-looking officer. Bert immediately recalled what Finch had said about Voss's guards being his enforcers and spies while he was in Penvellyn.

Bert struggled not to shake under the man's gaze.

'Well?' said the officer.

Bert heard a creak on the floor behind him.

'We were just getting some fresh . . .' The Professor trailed off.

Bert saw that the Professor had turned his shirt collar up, wrapped his sword up inside his coat and was walking with a stoop to appear older, but it wasn't much of a disguise.

'Is this your boy?' said the officer.

'Err . . . why, what did he do?' said the Professor.

'Nothing,' said the officer.

'Oh right, well then, yes, he's my son – I mean grandson,' said the Professor. 'Come along, boy.' He pushed Bert onwards and they walked down the aisle.

Bert could still feel the officer watching them, and tried not to look suspicious. The sun shone brightly through the windows and the soldiers shaded their eyes as they laughed and chatted to one another, but beneath it all Bert could sense something more serious. The officers seemed especially sombre as they muttered together over their game of cards.

He tripped over a scabbard as he passed their table.

'Watch yourself there,' said a nearby soldier.

'Keep moving,' muttered the Professor.

Bert passed a soldier who seemed to be briefing the others: 'All being well, we'll be flying out on the *Vulture* this evening,' said the man. 'They've got shrapnel netting prepared, like we asked. Two scout ships had their crews cleaned out over Cape Green last month.'

'Are the government really letting us go?' said another soldier. 'I heard there was going to be some kind of investigation, after, you know, the things that happened last time.'

The first man sneered. 'They can investigate if they want to,' he said. 'But Voss will find a way of getting us airborne. He always does. Just make sure to be alert for spies.'

Bert swallowed and shuffled by, trying to remain un-
obtrusive as he listened to the talk. He reached the exit,
opened the door, and slipped through. The Professor was
close behind him. Just then a soldier in the carriage began
to sing. The other men joined in:

> *You must pack up my belongings, love,*
> *And kiss me on the cheek,*
> *For I'm duty bound to leave this town,*
> *For the place beyond the sea . . .*

The Professor closed the door and the voices took on
an eerie note:

> *When the winter light is failing,*
> *With the children on your knee,*
> *Ask the band to play my favourite song,*
> *The place beyond the sea.*

Bert rested his back against the wall of the empty
carriage for a moment and breathed deeply. 'I thought
you said it was only going to be nannies aboard?' he said.

The Professor looked at his pocket watch. He seemed
to be assessing something. 'You can't plan for everything,'
he muttered. 'We might be late for our rendezvous.'

Bert checked his hand to make sure that the mark was

still calm. 'Professor,' he said. 'That blast that I created back at the bank. I didn't really know what I was doing.'

'Well, it certainly worked,' said the Professor.

'But, I mean – I don't how to control it,' said Bert. He wrapped the bandage up tight. 'What if something like that happens again? It might be dangerous.'

The Professor gave a hearty laugh. 'Well, you don't look too dangerous just yet,' he said. He continued in a kindly tone, 'It's lucky for us you had that power, Bert. You know, I've seen magic artefacts, like the legs I got for Finch, and I've seen some strange creatures in Ferenor. But I have to say, I've never seen anything like that blast at the bank. It's an impressive gift.'

Bert still felt uneasy. Finch's warning about the dangers of magic hovered at the back of his mind. It was hard not to keep checking the mark every few moments.

The Professor remained silent for a while. Rows of houses flashed by the window. The soldiers reached the end of their song. 'I know this isn't easy, Bert,' said the Professor. 'There's a lot we still need to work out about what's happened to you. And many more risks ahead, I expect. But the main thing for now is that we get you away from that madman Voss.'

'Finch mentioned the danger,' said Bert.

The Professor nodded. 'The man is obsessed with magic,' he said. 'He's made life very difficult for any pirates found carrying magic goods over the years. And there are some ugly rumours about his younger life – torturing and murdering people with any magical knowledge. I suspect that he wants to gain power from it somehow. He wouldn't be the first person to want to rekindle the old forces, and he has a good reason to need them, with the government in charge now, and the royals on the sidelines. And now you've appeared, wielding a power that was meant to have vanished from the world.' He sighed. 'I doubt Voss will take that well.'

Bert nodded. 'Is there really no one else with powers like this?' he said. 'I mean, I thought if this could happen to me, maybe there are other people that can use magic?'

'No,' said the Professor. 'The government might lie about magic artefacts, Bert, but what they say about mages is true. They've been dead and gone for two hundred years. There was supposed to have been a war that finished them off. It sounds like an ugly business.'

'Right,' said Bert. He swallowed. It was a lot to take in.

The Professor put his watch away and seemed to grow brighter again. 'I have to say, Bert, you're doing incredibly well for your first day as a pirate. You're a natural.'

Bert smiled despite himself. It occurred to him that he hadn't said thank you to the Professor for rescuing him, or for all the risks he was taking. 'Professor . . .' he began. He was interrupted by the sound of breaking glass in the carriage ahead of them.

'What was that?' said the Professor.

Bert peered ahead. From the entrance where they stood he could make out a long narrow corridor with doors on either side, apparently leading to private compartments. There was also a door for disembarking beside them. 'I don't think we're safe here,' said the Professor. He leant back and rubbed his brow. He seemed to be considering their options.

There was a grating sound coming from above them. They'd reached the cable-car section of the journey. Bert felt a strange weightlessness beneath his feet as the train lifted off the tracks and began to run down the metal cables that crossed over the Gulch. He looked outside and saw a hundred-foot drop on to black rocks. 'We're crossing over towards the port,' said Bert.

'Too late to jump train now,' said the Professor.

Chapter 9

Bert studied the surroundings of the carriage. It was a short, narrow space. Outside he could see the skyline of the city rising and falling with the sway of the cables. There was a deep valley of sharp black rocks beneath them, and a waterfall spilling from the cliffs across the way.

'Stay a few paces behind me, Bert,' said the Professor. 'I need to check on something.' He crept over to a doorway. There was a shadow at its base.

Bert was about to speak when the door burst open.

Cassius flew out of the compartment and tackled the Professor. There was a dull thud and a grunt of pain.

'Professor!' cried Bert. He rushed forwards to help.

'Stay back,' yelled the Professor. He dropped his weight on to Cassius's shoulders and heaved the quæstor down the corridor.

Cassius spun as he hit the wall. His hands flashed to his sides as he drew both his blades. 'Thought you'd got away, Roberts?' he said, as he lunged to attack.

The Professor drew his sword and performed a sweeping block. There was a sharp clang as one of Cassius's blades went spinning from his hand.

Cassius snarled and swung with his other sword.

The Professor ducked, then rushed close and grasped the quæstor by the wrist. He turned Cassius's remaining blade downwards and a drove it into the floor.

'Not like training, is it?' said the Professor.

Cassius cocked his elbow and struck the Professor on the chin. He gave a swipe of his other arm and the Professor's blade flew from his hand and embedded in the wall.

Bert again rushed forwards but a well-aimed kick knocked him back.

Both men flew into a flurry of blocks and punches. The air whistled with the speed of their blows and the carriage shook. Bert struggled to keep his footing.

Suddenly Cassius dropped low and kicked. He caught the Professor's heel and sent him staggering back. He hit the door of the carriage with a groan.

Cassius lunged forwards to grab him.

The Professor gripped the quæstor's arm and threw him full force against the door. There was a rending crash and both men disappeared through the opening.

'Professor!' cried Bert. He ran to the doorway and looked down. The drop below dizzied him for a moment but he forced himself to lean out.

He saw movement to his right. The Professor was hanging on to the side of the train. Cassius was luckier. He'd caught hold of a ladder, and was heading for the roof.

In that position, the Professor would be helpless.

Bert didn't have time to hesitate. He grabbed the sword that was embedded in the wall and threw himself up over the doorway. For a sickening moment he felt the headwind lifting his feet out into space but in a quick heave he managed to pull himself up on to the roof.

The cables creaked over his head as he crouched uneasily, trying to steady himself. The quæstor was only a short distance away over the carriage, shouting something that Bert couldn't hear. The Professor was still clinging desperately to the carriage side.

Cassius turned to face Bert.

'Get away from him,' yelled Bert.

The quæstor held out his hands. 'You don't have to do that, Bert.'

Bert glanced down at the Professor. It was clear that he couldn't get a foothold, that he was straining to cling on. 'Get back,' said Bert. He took a step forwards.

The quæstor didn't move.

'I'm warning you,' said Bert.

Cassius crouched lower to balance himself against the swaying of the carriage. 'It's over, Bert. I don't want to fight you, but I will if I have to.'

Bert gritted his teeth.

The quæstor took a step forwards. 'Give me the sword, or you'll get hurt,' he said. 'You've seen me fighting already. You know you're no match for me.'

Bert refused to give in. The sword shook in his hand. He could still hear the faint voices of the soldiers in the carriages below, singing another song.

Cassius took a step closer. 'This is your last warning.'

A hand shot over the side of the carriage. The blow hit Cassius's ankle and sent him tumbling backwards. His coat swirled around him as he rolled across the roof.

The Professor heaved himself up. 'Well done, Bert.'

'Look out!' said Bert.

Cassius was running to meet the Professor. The carriage swayed under them, and both men staggered. The Professor seemed to find his balance just in time.

'Take that!' yelled the Professor, swinging a punch.

Cassius took the impact and crumpled. He fell heavily

on to a wooden hatchway, and disappeared with a crash. There was a loud thump in the carriage below.

The Professor ran forwards, then froze. 'Oh dear,' he said.

Bert rushed over and peered down through the hole. Inside the carriage, a platoon of royal soldiers were staring up at them from around Cassius's collapsed form.

'What's going on here?' said a bemused-looking officer.

The Professor smiled. 'We had a disagreement over a seat.'

'Stay right there,' ordered the officer. 'Get them, men.'

'I think we'd better leave now,' said the Professor. He grabbed Bert and ran towards the front of the train. A pistol cracked behind them and a bullet hole appeared by their feet.

Bert raced as fast as he dared over the swaying roof.

The Professor took the sword from Bert's hands and put it into his belt. He nodded to a ladder that ran down the side of the carriage. 'Down there.'

'But we'll be sitting ducks,' said Bert.

'We've nearly reached land,' said the Professor. He pointed down the line of cables to a large wheat field. 'That's where we make our exit,' he said. 'If you're up to it, Bert?'

He was already swinging down on to the first rung.

Bert winced as he followed the Professor down the ladder. His bruises were still stiffening from the last fall. 'If I'm not, will you just throw me again?' he asked.

The Professor grunted by way of reply and lowered himself over the last handhold. The soldiers were shouting nearby. 'Make sure to roll,' the Professor said.

Bert looked down. It was a longer drop than he'd expected – three times his height – and the train was moving fast. When he looked to his side treetops flashed by at an alarming pace. 'What if I . . .?' he stopped speaking as the Professor dropped and landed with a rustle below.

'Come on, Bert!' yelled the Professor, his voice already fading into the distance.

Bert heard a shout of alarm in the corridor above. There were heavy footsteps heading towards him, followed by the drowsy voice of the quæstor.

'Wait,' shouted Cassius. 'Don't hurt the child.'

Bert swallowed. There were worse fears than a speeding fall right now. He looked down at the dizzying rows of wheat, gritted his teeth and jumped.

He hit the ground and sank into the wheat with a dull crunch. His head felt cloudy for a moment. He saw a pair of pale orbs peering out at him from a sea of darkness, and at the back of his mind he heard the angry voice of

Prince Voss, yelling: *'Find the boy! Find the boy!'*

'Bert,' called the Professor. 'Come on, we're not clear yet.'

Bert shook away the vision and started running.

Stalks of wheat poked through his clothes. The short stubble growth on the tracks of the field pierced his shoes and cut like splinters. But there was no chance of slowing down now. He kept his head forward and followed the Professor as they raced over the open space. He could hear the voices of soldiers in close pursuit. A whole troop of them seemed to have leapt from the train.

The Professor stopped suddenly.

'What is it?' asked Bert.

The Professor pointed ahead, where the field sloped down abruptly into a hollow that joined the boundaries of a large industrial complex. A thick smog hung over their view, but Bert could make out the jutting shapes of construction works and a tangle of wooden housing.

'The port's down there,' said the Professor.

'Which way do we go?'

'Straight through that factory.' The Professor shot forwards and began to bound and stumble down the steep bank into the smog.

Bert followed as fast as he dared, but his momentum soon took over, and he tumbled and rolled until he arrived at the bottom of the slope, caked in grass and mud. The Professor picked him up and helped him over a low metal fence. They landed on hard gravel. There were great vats of water on either side of them, with large crane-like girders hanging high above. A steady silver rain fell into the vats from a line of buckets, making a hissing and crackling sound as it hit.

'Bullet works,' said the Professor. He gestured to the machinery as he ran, apparently enjoying himself. 'It's clever stuff, Bert, for non-magic.'

Bert didn't have any breath left to respond. He pulled a stray stalk of wheat out of his collar and concentrated on moving his aching legs.

A workman up ahead yelled at them, and the Professor quickly cut between the vats and led Bert to a large hangar. 'Keep up,' he said.

'I'm trying,' panted Bert. His feet were lightened by fear. He could hear angry voices around the yard as they passed: calling out warnings or asking what they thought they were doing. They ran beneath a vast metal hull, ducked through a shower of orange sparks and arrived at a heavy latched doorway. The Professor knocked the latch open and beckoned.

Bert went inside and looked around. There was a straight corridor that led to the streets of the port. He was running for the light when a figure stepped into view at the end of the corridor. The figure was quickly joined by another. They were carrying swords.

'Soldiers,' cried Bert.

'Quick,' said the Professor. 'Go right.'

Bert tried a door by his side, found it unlocked and ran through. The Professor followed close behind. They passed over a metal walkway then down into a room filled with rubbish. The room ended in a series of large metal slides. There was no time to think. Bert jumped into the nearest shaft and slid down. His stomach lurched for a moment, then he hit the earth with a crunch and rolled on to his back. He was outside, in a pile of brittle clay and dirt. All around were stacks of waste metal, papers and manufacturing materials. It was all strangely familiar to him.

'Damn,' said the Professor. 'We're in the ratway.'

Bert looked around and nodded. Somehow he knew this place. Vague memories of early childhood came back to him – *dark times after someone had died, hiding in the shafts of the kilnworks, listening for someone returning.* 'Follow me,' he said. There were doorways and tunnels cut into the rubbish. A whole network of slums bordered the factory.

'You know your way?' asked the Professor in surprise.

Bert didn't say anything. He climbed up a flight of loose steps carved into the shale and cut through a tunnel made of rusted cans. At the end of the short enclosure he reached a straight narrow path that weaved between two metal fences. He could hear soldiers and workmen yelling to one another from around the yard. But he wasn't afraid of them here.

'Bert, do you know where we're going?' said the Professor.

Bert slowed his pace and crouched as something rattled the fence to his left. He heard a group of boots crunching through hard clay.

'There's a path here,' shouted a soldier. 'Let's climb up.'

Bert grabbed the Professor's sleeve, popped open a slat in the opposite fence and ran through a chicane of rotting wooden posts. The rubbish closed in around them as they ran, making an almost complete tunnel. They emerged at a flight of steps.

'Well done, Bert,' said the Professor, beaming.

The steps took them to a rickety rooftop overlooking the port. Bert caught a glimpse of docked sailing ships and the lazy shapes of airships floating over the waves.

There was a wooden bridge connecting them to the next rooftop. 'This way,' said the Professor. 'They should be able to pick us up from here.'

'But it's a dead end,' said Bert. He could hear officers yelling out orders from close behind, and soldiers calling in response. The troops seemed to be all around the block.

Pistols fired from the street below.

'Keep your head down, and keep up,' said the Professor. The bullets cracked as they passed. Bert ducked and ran with the Professor. They crossed over the bridge.

Ahead of them was a long flat roof.

'We can't stay up here,' said Bert.

'Do you hear that?' called the Professor over his shoulder.

Bert shook his head. His thoughts were filled with the volleys of gunshots and the drumming of his own heartbeat. 'Hear what?' he asked.

'You'll see,' said the Professor. He crouched, pulled a brass tube from his pocket and unscrewed the top. There was a crack like breaking glass and thick red smoke began to pour out of the container. He held it above his head and then tossed it down on to the gravel nearby.

Bert coughed. 'Is that a smoke screen?' he said.

'It's better than that,' said the Professor. 'It's a signal.'

'What kind of signal?'

A deep throbbing sound that Bert had been vaguely aware of before now grew suddenly louder and more intense. He looked towards the ocean. A huge green shape loomed over the rooftops. It was an airship. The sound of the engine grew to a deafening roar as its shadow fell over them. The bow guns fired, sending clouds of blue smoke all around the streets.

'That's the *Lugalbanda*,' said the Professor. 'My ship.'

Bert was stunned. Even in the fear and excitement, he felt a sense of wonder stirring inside him. The craving for adventure that he'd felt as a small child came to life again for one brilliant moment. But just then he heard something behind them. A running figure appeared through the smoke on the rooftop, drawing a sword and making straight for the Professor.

'Look out!' yelled Bert.

The Professor spun and raised his guard.

The soldier's weapon fell against the Professor's parrying blade, sending white sparks across the rooftop. The Professor twirled his grip over his head and attacked.

The soldier ducked and thrust one sword forwards while he blocked the blow with a dagger His lunge missed the Professor's stomach by inches. 'Surrender,' demanded the man.

Bert felt a heavy impact between his shoulders and tumbled to the ground. An officer grabbed and pinned him. In another moment metal handcuffs were forced on to his wrists. 'Let go of me,' he shouted in panic. He realized with a shock that there were soldiers all around. They raised their pistols and took aim at the Professor. Bert's heart turned cold.

'Ready,' said the officer. 'Shoot to kill.'

The Professor realized the danger too late. He

knocked down the soldier he was sword fighting then turned to see the row of weapons trained on him.

'Fire!' yelled the officer.

'No!' cried Bert. Time seemed to pass strangely. He felt a wave of energy in his palm and heard the rooftop creak beneath him. He placed his hand down on the rickety boards.

The rooftop exploded in a mass of dust and splinters.

He fell through the hole and the soldiers tumbled with him. A rotten wooden board snapped beneath his back and he fell again, hitting beams and debris as he went.

Then he struck the floor and lay still.

More soldiers were running over the rooftops above. Bert heard the clash of blades, and a strange swishing sound, like something flung through the air.

'He's getting away,' shouted an officer. 'Stop him!'

Bert caught a glimpse of the Professor swinging on the end of a rope. The airship soared away quickly, taking him well beyond the reach of the soldiers. It looked almost peaceful through the gap in the smoke. Then the wind changed and the view was obscured.

Bert was relieved that the Professor had escaped. But whatever elation he felt was short-lived. The soldiers were climbing out of the rubble around him.

'We've got him,' said one of the men. 'He's in here.'

'Put your hands up,' yelled a gruff voice.

Bert glanced around and saw that he was surrounded. Men were climbing through the window of the ruined wall of the building, training their guns on him.

He stood unsteadily on the crumbling wreckage, covered in dirt and debris, assessing his cuts and bruises. An upright beam seemed to offer a handhold, but a soldier pushed him away and told him to stand against the wall. 'All right,' Bert said, raising his hands. 'I surrender.'

It seemed unreal. He thought back to his cosy dormitory at school, his collection of toys and magazines, the pillow that had grown shaped to his head, and then further into the past, to a vague memory of his home as a small child, someone ruffling his hair and putting him to bed.

He wished he could remember them clearly, see their faces and hear the words they'd said, but it was like there was a barrier in his mind separating him from those memories. There was no familiar warmth to be found in the world any more. The soldiers barked orders at him and seized his handcuffs. His stomach sank as they led him out into the sunlight and he saw Prince Voss standing with his arms folded. It occurred to him that he had made a terrible, irreversible mistake.

Chapter 10

B ert opened his eyes. It took him a moment to realize where he was, but gradually the details returned to him: the soldiers forcing him into the battle wagon; the rushed journey through the town with the doctor at his side; and now this – the bare prison cell and the barred window. His bandaged hand was encased in a metal glove and his ankle was chained to the bed.

He remembered the words of the prison warden as they'd thrown him into his cell: 'I hear you have had some luck as an escape artist. Let me tell you this: there is no escape from my prison. We have the best guards, the best reinforced doors, unbreakable locks, double rows of walls and fences, and we are surrounded by an impassable moat. Your cell is six storeys up. Even if you could get through the window – which is impossible – you would fall to your death. You'd better get used to the idea of staying here, because the only ways to leave are release, or death.'

Bert understood the hopelessness of his predicament. He knew the reputation of Grimwater Prison: the place where the worst criminals were kept. But he still had to get out. It wasn't just that he was terrified of what would happen; he was determined not to let Voss win. The man clearly had some terrible plan in mind. Bert didn't want to help him gain power.

He raised his hand and tried to will the energy to strike at the door, but nothing happened. He didn't know if it was the metal glove, or something lacking in his strength, but he couldn't seem to create the same power any more. He raised his hand again. He tried to make himself angry, jumped up and down, imagined Prince Voss standing there. Nothing worked.

He rested his head in his hands and tried to keep down his despair. Even the air in prison seemed harder to breathe than the air outside. Every noise was harsh and threatening.

There was a knock at the door, and the lock turned.

'You're to come with me,' said the prison guard. 'Put

your hands on your head while I restrain you.' He entered the cell and opened a pair of manacles.

'Where are you taking me?' asked Bert.

The man took the heavy metal from Bert's palm, then snapped the manacles over his wrists and detached the chain from the bed. 'You're going to meet Prince Voss,' he said, giving the chains a cruel tug.

It was obvious to Bert that the guards were afraid of him. But he sensed a deeper fear in the man's voice when he mentioned the prince. The thought made him shudder.

The man took him down the corridor from the cell to a room with a thick metal door. He unlocked the door and pushed Bert inside. It was a small, plain room. There was a desk, two chairs and what looked like a tall case of files. There didn't appear to be anyone inside.

'The prisoner to see you, Prince Voss,' said the guard.

'Thank you,' said Voss, as he stepped out from behind the case of files. He was wearing a black cape along with his royal uniform. It looked like something an executioner would wear. Even in such a small room, he still had his sword strapped to his waist. He looked coldly at Bert for a moment before addressing the guard again. 'You may leave us,' he said.

Bert felt a chill. He wondered if Voss intended to kill him.

The guard gave a salute and stepped through the door. The heavy lock turned with a clank and the room was sealed. There was no other way out.

Voss gestured to the empty seats. 'Be comfortable,' he said.

Bert looked down at his manacles and wondered exactly how he was supposed to do that. But he took his seat anyway.

Voss sat across from him. 'Do you know why you're here?'

Bert wasn't sure how to reply.

'I've been reading notes on you,' said Voss. 'Not that there's much left after that fire destroyed your school records.' He stared blankly at Bert. 'I hear you're an orphan.'

Bert nodded. 'I never knew my parents.'

The Prince gave a dismissive wave of his hand. 'That shouldn't trouble you,' he said. 'My mother died when I was born, and my father, well – he doesn't like me very much.' He looked down at the desk and clenched his fist. 'Do you know who my father is?'

Bert felt this was an obvious question. 'King Eldred?'

'Eldred, King of Penvellyn,' said Voss. 'Not that it means much any more. The old man is so weak he can barely get out of bed these days, and everyone knows that the government has all the real power. We just have a little money, and a little influence – and the odd prison. I suppose in a few more years they might get rid of us completely – for the sake of a modern, neater world.' He shook his head. 'But if I could show them what a real leader could do, then perhaps they might change their mind. That would truly be something special, wouldn't it?'

Bert felt it was safest to agree. 'I suppose,' he said.

Voss nodded. 'I know a way to get *real* power,' he said. 'I've studied all my life to find a way of surpassing even the most powerful kings of Penvellyn. But there's something stopping me.'

'What?' asked Bert.

'You,' said Voss.

Bert felt a chill. 'I don't understand.'

Voss's expression darkened. 'I'm getting to that part,' he said. 'You see, you happened to interfere with one of my experiments, a very important experiment at the museum.'

'I don't understand,' repeated Bert.

'Guard,' yelled Voss. 'Bring in the doctor.'

The door opened and the guard shoved a nervous-looking man into the room. Bert recognized him as the doctor he'd seen in his vision at the museum.

'Explain it to him,' ordered Voss.

The doctor looked confused. 'Explain?' he said. His gaze fell on Bert, and he gave a start. 'You're –you're the boy.' He wiped his forehead. 'How did you activate it?'

'I don't understand,' said Bert.

'Has the spirit spoken to you yet?' asked the doctor.

'What spirit?'

The doctor looked nervously at Voss.

'Tell him,' said Voss.

The doctor swallowed and took a few breaths. 'That mirror you saw is an old summoning device, made in Ferenor. It's supposed to bring a spirit, made of magic energy, into our world. It's how the mages got their power, back in the old days.'

The doctor glanced at Voss again.

'Go on,' said Voss. 'Before I get impatient.'

The doctor wiped more sweat from his brow. 'Spirits bond with a particular mage when they enter our world. They need the energy of that person to survive in this environment, and the person, in turn, gets some of the powers of the spirit. It's sort of collaborative. They can even see each other's thoughts from time to time – like they're sharing the same space.'

Bert remembered the voice he had heard back at the bank, and the strange visions he'd had. What the doctor said made sense, but he tried not to show any reaction.

'We had the mirror,' continued the doctor. 'The prince retrieved it from Ferenor, along with a lot of research about how it's supposed to work. We thought that if we followed the ritual, the spirit would have to come through the mirror. And then we would be prepared to trap it before it bonded with anyone. Once we captured it, we could use its power—'

'That part is not important,' interrupted Voss.

The doctor paused. 'Of course, Your Highness,' he said. He looked at Bert again. 'The point is, we did everything we were supposed to do to summon a spirit, but it didn't work. I thought that was the end of it. Maybe it was a myth after all. We kept the mirror set up with the capturing device in place, just in case something happened over time. But I didn't hold out much hope.'

Voss tapped his fingers loudly on the desk.

'Then the mirror started glowing,' the doctor went on. 'I realized that something strange was going on but we weren't sure what. To begin with, I thought we might have been tricked by the spirit. There are stories about them being able to control people's minds and alter their perception of reality. I thought maybe it *had* appeared but we just hadn't seen it.' He rubbed his hands together nervously and looked at Voss for approval. 'Then we heard about what happened to you at the museum. I thought, *What if the spirit had arrived, but not through our mirror?* We hadn't anticipated that eventuality but I knew there was a mirror in the museum collection that we'd previously dismissed from our research. After I heard what had happened there, it seemed to make sense. But if the spirit came into the world without being captured, it must have bonded with someone.'

Bert tried to keep his expression level, but he could sense that the doctor had hit upon the truth. Whatever this spirit was, he'd certainly seen its effects.

'And there's more,' said the doctor. 'We might not have captured the spirit, but if we could find out who it is connected to we could still trap it in our world and use its energy—'

'I had another question for you, Doctor,' interrupted Voss.

The man flinched. 'Yes?'

'When you realized the boy had been affected by the mirror, why did you contact the pirate Roberts and give him a key to my vault at Hammerton National Bank?'

The doctor turned pale but he managed to hold the prince's gaze. For the first time, Bert saw determination in his face. 'I see,' he began, his voice shaking, 'I did that, Your Highness, because I know that you are planning to use the power of the spirit for something terrible. And as soon as I realized there was a chance you might succeed, I knew I had to stop you.'

Voss's face trembled with rage. He slipped off his gloves and Bert was stunned to see a shining metal fist where his right hand would have been. The metal was the same hue as Finch's legs and the fingers flexed in perfect imitation of life. Voss suddenly slammed the fist into the wall, pulled out a chunk of stone and threw it at the doctor. 'Traitor!' he yelled.

The stone struck the man to the floor.

'Guards!' The door was hastily opened from outside. 'Take him away,' roared Voss. 'Execute him immediately.'

A guard rushed in and began to drag the doctor from the room, but the doctor blinked and looked at Bert before he left. 'Don't help him,' he whispered. 'The weapon . . .'

Voss pushed the doctor from the room and slammed the door. He breathed heavily for a few moments and looked at the floor. 'Why must there be so many traitors?' he muttered. He staggered back to his desk and replaced his gloves carefully, covering his metal hand again. 'Enough,' he said as he stood up straight. 'Let's begin the real interrogation.' He took up a small, dark crystal from his desk and strode towards Bert. Something about the object filled Bert with dread. 'This is an artefact I found in the far north of Ferenor. Do you recognize it?' He paused. 'Do you notice anything strange about it?'

Bert didn't reply – he was still shocked by what had happened to the doctor, and by the frightening power of Voss's metal hand.

'I'll ask you again,' said Voss. 'Have you seen the spirit?'

Bert's voice shook. 'I don't know what you mean.'

Voss sighed. 'Very well,' he said. He held the crystal closer to Bert. It glowed with a strange green light. 'Then we will try this experiment.'

Bert began to feel uncomfortable. The mark on his hand burnt and his arm felt cold. He looked down and saw an inky black stain spreading over this skin.

'It's working, isn't it?' asked Voss.

Bert winced in pain. 'What are you doing to me?'

'This is the final part of the puzzle,' said Voss. He stepped closer and held out the crystal. His face was set with determination. 'That is how I will capture it from you, Bert.'

The world seemed to spin. Bert felt the pain from somewhere distant as the coldness travelled up his arm. It was like he was leaving his own body. 'Stop,' he said. 'It hurts.'

Voss didn't seem to be listening. 'Why doesn't it appear?' His voice grew angrier. 'If it needs his energy to survive, why doesn't it try to protect him?'

There was a long pause.

Bert felt warmth returning to him and when he opened his eyes he saw that Voss had taken the dark crystal away. His arm still hurt, but the black marks were receding.

Voss looked down at him with obvious disgust. 'Why

would it choose you?' he said. 'A weakling child? It is as if it wants to fail.' He clapped his hands suddenly.

A guard entered and went to grab Bert's marked arm, recoiled, and grabbed Bert's other arm instead.

'Consider this,' said Voss. 'I am not without mercy. If you can find a way to assist me in capturing this spirit, we could be friends. If not, I will continue the same experiment from today, day after day, until I have it in my power.' He went over to his desk and tapped the dark crystal that rested there. 'I have complete power over this prison,' he said. 'It's not just you that I can trap here. You should think of your friends, too.' He gestured to the guard.

The guard gave a quick salute and led Bert back to the door. Bert's body ached, but the long grey corridor and the heavy metal doors seemed almost pleasant after the pain and fear of the interrogation room. He tried not to think about what was happening to the doctor. He couldn't forget how frightened the man had looked, or the terrible suddenness of Voss's anger.

He shook his head and thought over what the doctor had said about the spirit. It was a lot to take in, but he began to wish desperately that it would appear. It seemed like his only hope.

Chapter 11

Bert's cell was dark when the guard pushed him inside. He recalled the threat Voss had made when he left the room. He didn't understand what the prince meant exactly, about hurting other people. He didn't have any family to care for and as far as he knew the Professor and Finch had got away.

Then a shadow moved across the room.

'Who's there?' said Bert.

'Oh, hello,' said a familiar voice. Norton stepped forward out of the gloom. 'I was wondering when you'd be back. It's not the nicest of places, is it?'

'Norton?' yelled Bert. For a moment, he was too stunned to take it in. He felt like he was in a strange dream. 'What on earth are you doing here?'

Norton shrugged. 'I must be in trouble.'

'But . . . why?'

'I don't know,' said Norton. His face looked blank for a moment while he was thinking. 'I suppose they must have imagined we're working together.'

When the shock faded, Bert felt a wave of horror. He thought of Voss's threat. Was it possible he had brought Norton here because he was Bert's only friend?

'You have to get them to release you,' said Bert. 'You can't be locked up in this place, just because of me.' The more impassive Norton looked, the sadder Bert felt. He threw himself down on the bed and stared at the ceiling. 'I just can't believe they would do this.'

'It certainly makes you think,' said Norton.

For a while they were both silent.

'How did your interrogation go?' asked Norton.

Bert couldn't help feeling that Norton didn't appreciate the gravity of the situation. You might ask how an exam went, or a walk to the shops, but not an interrogation.

'It went about as well as you'd expect,' said Bert.

'What did he want?'

'Apparently, he wants to be my friend.'

'That's nice,' said Norton.

'Not really,' said Bert. 'He said I've stolen power from

one of his experiments, and I get the impression he wants it back.' He looked down at his hand and explained to Norton everything that the doctor had told him about the spirit. There was no point in keeping secrets now. Norton received the information as unemotionally as if Bert was talking about the weather.

When Bert had finished, Norton said: 'I think they're wrong.'

'About what?'

'About being able to control this spirit,' said Norton. 'I mean, it's meant to be powerful, and I suppose it's clever. Why would they think they could trick it?'

'They seemed pretty confident.'

'I don't think they know what they're doing,' said Norton.

Bert took some comfort in Norton's words. He lay on the hard cot that served as his bed and clutched his aching arm. 'I hope you're right,' he said. 'Thank you, Norton.' He closed his eyes, and tucked his clothes tight around himself. Exhaustion pulled him down.

He dreamt that he was walking down a country lane. There were birds singing in the hedgerows and white clouds drifting by. The sun felt warm on his shoulders. A tree seemed to offer a good place to climb for a better view. Its branches hung low, almost in his grasp.

But when he raised his hand he heard a rattle of metal.

He woke feeling depressed. There was a tray holding a bowl of gruel on the floor. He didn't even have the will to inspect it. He began to sense that he was here for good, or until Voss got what he wanted. It was hard to keep down a wave of despair.

Norton was sitting on the floor, tracing shapes in the dust.

'What are you drawing?' said Bert.

'Just clouds,' said Norton. 'They're not very good though.'

'What do you mean?'

'They look more like, just, shapes.'

'Clouds *are* just shapes, Norton.'

Norton looked glum. 'Well, I don't know what's wrong with them then.'

Bert sat up and tried to clear his head. He was already dreading the next meeting with Voss. His only thought was that somehow he had to find a way to escape. Today he was going to study the walk from the cell, in case there was some weakness he'd missed. His hand gave a twinge, and he looked down at it. He wondered again if the spirit really could help him.

'Do you believe in all this stuff, Norton?' said Bert.

'What?'

'Magic, and spirits and things,' said Bert. He went over

to the bowl of gruel. 'You didn't seem that surprised when I talked about it yesterday. You just, sort of, accepted it.'

Norton continued drawing in the dust. 'It's not really a question of believing, is it?' he said. 'I mean, if it's happening to you, it's happening to you, and that's that.'

Bert puzzled over this statement while he poked at the gruel with his spoon. He couldn't find any fault in Norton's reasoning exactly, but it didn't answer his question.

Something crinkled under the food bowl.

He reached down and pulled out a piece of paper. He unfolded it to find a note: *Jailbreak, tonight, midnight – be ready to leave.*

Bert's heart began to beat faster. He read the note over a few times before the words really sank in. 'Norton, you should look at this,' he said. 'I think someone's trying to help us.'

Norton looked at the note dubiously. 'It could be a joke.'

'A joke?'

'You know, like, from the prison guards. It would be quite funny, if you think about it. Just to put a note in someone's cell that said "jailbreak" – and then nothing happens.'

Bert frowned. 'You really are the worst sometimes,

Norton. Of course it's not a joke. You'd have to be completely insane to do something like that.'

'Sorry,' said Norton. 'What are you going to do?'

Bert was already peering around the cell for any other scraps of paper or other new objects. But there didn't appear to be any further clues. 'We're going to be ready,' he said. He sat down on the bed and took a few deep breaths. The only problem now was waiting for midnight. There was no clock in the place. The window was dark but he couldn't guess how much of the night remained.

He spent a long time thinking over how the jailbreak would happen. It must be someone inside the prison that was going to help them. They had left the note in his cell, after all. That meant it was probably a prison guard. Unless one of the prisoners had managed to sneak around the building? But then, how had they found him, and why would they help?

He was still thinking it over when he heard footsteps.

'This is it,' he whispered to Norton. 'Be ready.'

Norton didn't appear ready. He was lying on the floor with his ankles crossed and his hands behind his head. He didn't even seem particularly awake.

The lock in the door rattled.

'We're in here,' whispered Bert.

A confused-looking guard opened the door. 'I know

you're in there,' he said, harshly. 'I've come to collect you for interrogation. You're to speak with Prince Voss immediately.'

Bert's legs felt heavy with fear as the guard marched him down the corridor towards the interrogation room. For a short time he still held out hope that this could be a trick – that the guard would reveal himself to be a friend at the last moment. But he had no such luck.

The guard shoved him inside the room. 'The prisoner, Prince Voss.'

Voss nodded. He was seated as before, as if he hadn't moved during the intervening hours. The guard saluted and then left the room, locking the door behind him.

Bert felt utterly miserable.

'Have you thought about my offer?' asked Voss.

'I don't understand what the offer is,' said Bert. The fear of what lay ahead and his bitter disappointment that this wasn't the jailbreak made him feel bold enough to speak his mind.

'You heard the doctor mention a weapon?' said Voss.

Bert said nothing.

'He always thought I was crazy,' said Voss. 'I suppose it was useful in a way. If he really believed I could do it, perhaps he would never have helped me.'

'What do you expect me to do?' said Bert.

'You have a bond with this spirit, Bert,' said Voss. 'I know that you've already used its powers in your foolish attempt to escape capture. Now, I want you to make it appear.'

Bert gritted his teeth and said nothing. He knew that he wanted to call for help more than anything right now. But he was determined not to assist Voss, whatever the cost.

Voss looked at him blankly. 'It won't help to defy me,' he said. 'I know more about spirits than anyone else in the modern world. I've studied every collection of writing that exists on the subject.' He opened a drawer of the desk and took out the dark crystal again. 'In fact, this whole idea of trapping the spirit wasn't mine – it was a technique that used to belong to some very nasty mages who lived in the wastes in the north of Ferenor.' He flicked the crystal into the air and caught it. 'If a spirit wouldn't choose to help them, this was their solution. I admire their way of thinking.' He tapped his fingers on the table. 'It is a proven method, you see. It will work.'

Bert remained silent. He had the impression that Voss was testing him, trying to make him feel threatened. Perhaps he thought that it would make the spirit appear.

'Do you think I'm crazy, too?' said Voss. He held the crystal a little closer to Bert, and turned it over in his fingers. 'My father used to say that I was crazy . . .'

Bert was distracted by something that appeared in the corner of his vision. For a moment he thought he was seeing things. It looked as if a figure had just emerged through the wall of the room. It was shrouded in black and seemed to hover just above the ground.

'Are you listening to me?' asked Voss. 'There is no point in your protecting this thing. It is using your energy to stay alive in our world. It is a leech—'

He was interrupted by a burst of light.

The dark crystal flashed out of his hand and shot away over the floor.

'*What?*' yelled Voss. He leapt up in surprise.

The spirit drifted out of the wall.

Bert stared at the apparition in amazement. It moved quickly over the room and seemed to draw the shadows with it. As it came closer he felt the power building in his palm. The energy seemed to flow over his manacles and the metal turned cold.

'Guards!' cried Voss. 'Guards, get in here.'

Bert heard a thump, and realized with a start that the manacles and restraints had fallen from his wrists. He ran for the door and raised his hand on instinct.

A guard entered the room.

A blast exploded from Bert's palm and knocked the guard off his feet. The man hit the wall and slumped down, unmoving. His keys jangled on to the floor.

Bert quickly scooped them up.

Voss was too occupied with the spirit to intervene. The thing hovered over the room like a small storm. Voss leapt away and snatched up the crystal.

'Now!' he yelled as he held it up at the spirit.

The crystal glowed with a sickening green light. But the prince wasn't fast enough – the spirit flowed away into the wall and disappeared.

'You think you can escape?' asked Voss. He glanced again at Bert, and seemed to realize for the first time that the boy had escaped from his restraints.

Bert grasped the keys tight. For a moment fear paralysed him. He was terrified of facing Voss's anger, but he knew this was his only chance.

'Give those to me,' said Voss.

Bert ran through the door, slammed it shut behind him, and turned the key in the lock. There was a thump on the other side. Voss began to yell furiously but the sound was muffled. There was only one door into the room. As far as Bert knew he had the only key.

He'd locked the prince up in his own prison.

He gave a brief chuckle of satisfaction. But the thought of the task that lay ahead brought him back to reality. He dismissed any thoughts of the spirit for now. Whatever its intention, he couldn't waste time worrying. 'I've got to get to Norton,' he muttered.

He ran down the corridor to his cell and turned the lock. For a moment he was confused. Norton didn't appear to be there. Then suddenly his friend stepped into view.

Bert flinched in surprise.

'Are you all right?' asked Norton.

'You scared me, hiding in the shadows like that,' said Bert. He laughed a little shakily. 'You won't believe what I just saw back there.' He explained as quickly as he could what had happened in the interrogation room, still feeling unnerved. 'It must be nearly midnight,' he said. 'But we can't wait around here. It's only a matter of time before someone finds Voss.'

'But where should we go?'

'Anywhere,' said Bert. He led Norton out of the cell and looked to the left. That appeared to be the only option, other than heading back to the interrogation room. He could still hear Voss hammering on the door. Each impact jarred his nerves. 'Come on,' he said.

Somewhere above them he heard a clock chiming midnight. But he didn't feel like he could just sit and wait in his cell, with Voss so close at hand and the chance of discovery increasing with each passing moment. He forced himself to peek around the next corner.

He caught his breath and leant back. There were two guards with swords standing just a few paces from him.

There was no way he'd be able to pass without being seen. A panic began to grow inside him. This was his best chance to get out. He would have to try and run for it.

Just then there was a heavy thump from around the corner and a clatter as a sword fell to the floor. Bert dared to peer out from his hiding place.

The guards were both lying on the floor, unconscious.

Finch stood over them, patting her hands. 'Now, which way?' she muttered.

Bert was too stunned to speak.

Finch spotted him and gave a jump of alarm. 'You?' she said.

'How did you get here?' said Bert.

Norton sighed. 'How did any of us get here?'

'I broke in,' said Finch.

Bert was about to explain that he had broken out when he heard a clang from the far end of the corridor. A hole appeared in the door of the interrogation room and a metal hand reached through the gap. 'You think that you can hold me in my own prison?' roared Voss.

Finch stared at the metal hand with obvious interest. 'Who's in there?'

'Guards,' bellowed Voss from inside the room. 'Stop them.'

Heavy footsteps were converging on their location. Bert grabbed Finch's hand. 'We can talk about all this later,' he said. 'We need to find a way out.'

They ran together down the corridor, heading away from the footsteps and back towards Bert's cell. 'Do you have a plan of escape?' asked Bert.

'I have a rough idea,' said Finch. She gave a grin that reminded Bert of her father.

A guard appeared from another doorway. 'Stop!' he yelled.

'Do we stop or not?' said Norton.

Finch ducked away from the guard's first clumsy swing and kicked the man's knee, then spun and fired her other foot into his stomach.

The man flew back along the corridor and landed heavily.

'I suppose not, then,' said Norton.

Bert heard the click of a gun hammer being drawn behind them. He turned just in time to see a guard aiming a pistol at Finch's back. Again, an instinct told him to raise his right hand.

The power burned in his palm. The pistol sprang away from the guard and flew into Bert's grasp. He looked down stupidly at the weapon.

'Get the light,' said Finch.

Bert saw what she meant. He aimed at the nearest lantern and fired. The pistol kicked in his hand and the glass lantern shattered, spilling burning amphor across the corridor.

They ran from the fire to the open cell door.

Finch frowned. 'How did you get the gun?'

Bert shook his head. 'My hand – it just happened.'

Finch ducked into the cell and pulled a brass cylinder from her pocket. 'I need to ready the signal.'

Bert crouched with her and Norton stood beside them. A shot rang out and shattered a tile on the wall beside them. The corridor filled with smoke from the burning amphor. They began to cough. 'I thought this place couldn't look any worse,' said Norton.

Bert could hear more guards approaching. It looked like they had the three of them trapped. He felt terrible. 'Finch,' he said. 'I'm sorry about this. You should run if you can.'

Finch frowned and said nothing. She bit the brass cylinder and twisted, then shoved it between the window bars. A cloud of red smoke spilt out with a dull hiss.

Bert coughed as smoke filled the room from both directions. 'What's that for?'

Finch pointed upwards. For a moment Bert didn't understand what she was getting at, but then he heard a dull rumbling sound.

'What's that?' said Norton.

'Something flying, I think,' said Bert.

Finch frowned again. Bert heard a crack that sounded

like a gunshot and a distant yell of alarm.

The engine seemed to be directly overhead.

'Airship,' muttered Bert.

Finch grabbed him and crouched low.

The wall suddenly burst and crumbled. A huge crack appeared in the masonry and the smell of gun smoke filled the room. There was another loud bang and the Professor appeared, swinging a large sledgehammer and looking thoroughly pleased with himself.

'Thank goodness we got the right cell,' he said. He swung down from a rope and landed in the middle of the floor. Bert could make out the looming hull of the airship lowering into view outside. The cannons were firing coloured flare charges all over the prison.

Guards were yelling, and alarms sounded.

Bert helped Norton to his feet.

'Not an easy descent,' said the Professor. 'Good to see you're not too worse for wear.' He looked at the open door, and Bert's unmanacled hands. 'Well done, Finch,' he said. 'I'm impressed you found your way.' He took a crossbow from his shoulder and loaded a grapple.

'There's nothing wrong with my sense of direction,' said Finch.

Bert pointed at the crossbow. 'What's that for?' he said.

'I swung down here,' said the Professor. 'But it would

take too long to climb up.' The airship was slightly below them now, hovering in the darkness. The Professor aimed the crossbow and fired. A rope went hissing into the night, and the crossbow grapple lodged in the airship's rigging. There was a wide gap between the wall and the ship.

The Professor slung a metal chain over the rope.

'You'd better go first,' said the Professor. 'Hold on tight, and it will slide you right on to the deck. Let go, and it's a long way down. My men will catch you at the other side.'

Bert looked back to make sure Norton was with him and then took hold of the chain. He stood on the edge of the six-storey drop. The ground below seemed to swim in his vision.

'Take your time,' said the Professor. 'No rush.'

Bert suddenly remembered the Professor's tricks. 'Don't push—'

But it was too late. The Professor shoved him out into space.

Bert's stomach lurched and the airship rushed towards him. He could make out figures on the deck reaching for him. The tangle of ropes shot into view.

He hit the netting with a thump and felt strong arms pulling him down to safety. In another moment he was on the deck, breathing heavily but otherwise unhurt.

Norton landed beside him and muttered something about feeling dizzy. He staggered over to the edge of the deck as the Professor and Finch slammed into the rigging.

'Well done everyone,' said the Professor. 'You actually caught us.'

Finch cut the rope away. 'We're detached,' she said.

'Get us away from here, Mr Peel,' yelled the Professor.

'Yes, sir,' called a grizzled-looking man at the ship's controls.

The engines of the airship rose to a roar and the deck swayed beneath Bert's feet. He could see the lights of the prison fading behind them and the occasional flash as a guard fired a shot. But the bullets came nowhere near. The full sense of triumph didn't sink in until Finch helped him to his feet and led him to the front of the ship. 'Welcome aboard,' she said.

Bert laughed and looked down. He saw the world sailing swiftly beneath them. The trees looked like little models in the moonlight, and the clouds were close enough to touch. 'So this is what it feels like?' he said. He looked around the airship and the smiling crew. He was free.

Chapter 12

The following morning Bert sat in the Professor's cabin, wearing an oversized woollen jumper over his regular school shirt and trousers, giving an account of the prison to Finch and her father. Through the rear windows the ocean passed peacefully below.

'The doctor was executed?' said the Professor.

Bert nodded grimly.

'It's a shame,' said the Professor. 'It was brave of him to contact me the way he did. I'm sorry I didn't explain earlier, Bert. I was trying to protect the two of you.'

'Did he tell you about the spirit?' asked Bert.

'No. I suppose he didn't have the opportunity to sneak

a longer message to me. He just sent me the key to Voss's vault and instructions to get you away from Penvellyn as soon as possible.' He rubbed his chin. 'I also suspect he didn't know exactly what Voss is planning with the spirit. You mentioned something about a weapon?'

'That's what he told me,' said Bert. 'Just before they took him away.'

The Professor nodded. 'I suppose that makes more sense than Voss wanting to gain magic powers himself. I mean, no offence, Bert, but taking on the powers you have wouldn't exactly make him an unstoppable force. There has to be something more.'

'He *is* crazy, though,' said Finch.

'Good point,' said the Professor.

'There was something else,' said Bert. 'He said he wanted to capture the spirit in this dark crystal It sounded like that was what he was planning all along.'

'That sounds troubling,' said the Professor. He looked out the window. 'Anyway, Bert, it's good to have you back with us. I would never live it down with my crew if I'd let you save my life like that and then left you to rot in Grimwater Prison.'

Bert nodded. 'Thank you. I don't know what would have happened if I'd stayed. But how did you know where to find me? Did the doctor tell you that too?'

'No,' said the Professor. 'I don't believe he could have

smuggled out another note, or planned a jailbreak. And the method of contacting us was different.'

'We landed at one of our pirate havens,' explained Finch. 'And there was a messenger pigeon waiting for us. It had a note that told us which cell you were in and when to rescue you.'

Bert was confused. 'So we don't know who helped me?'

'There can't be a shortage of people that hate Prince Voss,' said the Professor. 'I suppose another one of his men is trying to get in the way of his schemes. Good luck to them, I say.'

Finch nodded. They didn't appear overly concerned.

Bert was uneasy about their complacency. The more he thought about Voss's words, the more he sensed a wider danger. 'We have to stop him,' he said.

The Professor glanced at Finch. 'I'm not sure we want to pick a fight with the man in line for the throne of Penvellyn just now, if we can help it, Bert.'

'But he's already picked a fight with us,' said Bert. 'We can't let him do what he wants. If he catches this spirit, and uses it with this weapon, something terrible might happen. And if he wants to catch the spirit, he has to catch me too.' He shuddered. 'I don't think he'll just give up.'

'Well, you're not wrong there, Bert,' said the Professor. 'Voss is almost certainly chasing us. And he has a very good airship with which to do it. All I mean to say is, we shouldn't actively look for a fight with him right now if we can help it. Our priority is to find out what's happened to you, and see if we can fix it. I'm pleased to say we've made some progress.'

Bert leant forward as the Professor opened a file.

'These are from the notes you stole from Hammerton National Bank,' said the Professor. 'The doctor directed us to these for a reason. I don't think he knew what Voss was aiming to do with the spirit exactly, but he seemed to think it would help to find out where Bert's mirror came from. These records explain which adventurer found the mirror and brought it to Penvellyn. If we can gather their version of events, we stand a much better chance of understanding it.'

'But who found it?' said Bert.

'That's where things get tricky,' said the Professor. 'Captain Amleth, the legendary early explorer of Ferenor ruins, was the one who found the mirror. It seems it was one of the last things he ever did. He went out on a return voyage and never came back.'

'Do the notes say where he found it?' asked Bert.

'No,' said the Professor. 'But I think we can do better than that. I know where Captain Amleth's airship crashed. It's in a remote region of Ferenor – the Sethera Mountains.'

Bert was confused. 'But if the captain is dead, and his ship is gone, how are we supposed to find out where he got the mirror? Doesn't that mean the secret is lost for good?'

'Actually, no,' said the Professor. 'You see, Bert, all captains keep notes about their adventures in a ship's safe. No one has ever searched the wreck of the *Erebus* – Amleth's ship. If we can find those notes, we should be able to find all of the information we need. He was the greatest adventurer of his time. He might even know more about this business than Voss.'

Bert nodded. 'Why has no one searched the wreck before?'

The Professor glanced at Finch. 'Well, it's not exactly an easy place to get to. There are crosswinds that make it impossible to land an airship. And the forests below are impassable – the further we stay away from them the better. It's not going to be easy getting down there—'

'Also, the ship's haunted,' interrupted Finch.

The Professor looked annoyed. 'It's *supposed* to be haunted,' he said. 'I'm not convinced that anyone has got down there to find out. Probably just aeronauts' tales.'

Bert wasn't convinced. Something in the Professor's tone suggested he was trying to play down the danger. But he couldn't help being excited about the prospect ahead – it felt like he was going on his first real adventure.

'How long until we get there?' he said.

'We'll be at the Ferenor coast in a few hours,' said the Professor. 'After that, it depends what the weather is like. I think we'll be over the Sethera Mountains by this afternoon.'

Bert nodded. 'And I can search the wreck with you?'

The Professor looked unsure.

'He's done fine so far,' said Finch. 'And he has more at stake than any of us.'

Bert was pleased to have her support.

'All right,' said the Professor. 'I was thinking of taking you with us anyway.' He rubbed his chin and looked at the map again. 'But it will be a dangerous landing. I'd better start planning.'

Bert was thrilled. 'What should I do in the meantime?'

'You can do some research,' said the Professor. 'We're going to be crossing the coast of Ferenor very soon, but there's a little time to see if you can dig up anything about spirits or mirrors from the ship's library.' He nodded to Finch. 'If you can remember where that is?' he asked, with a grin.

Finch gave the door of the library a strong kick and a waft of stale air rushed out to meet them. There were book-shelves running all around the small cabin, with strings lashed across to stop the books falling out. Bert ran his finger across the nearest set of spines and read the titles. He was surprised to find that Norton was already sitting there, in the dark, holding a book.

'How can you read in this light?' asked Bert.

Norton shrugged. 'Some poetry you can just feel.'

Bert couldn't help pulling a face, but he was glad that Norton didn't seem to have been affected by his time in prison. In fact, he seemed more like himself than ever.

'There,' said Finch, igniting the amphor lamp.

Norton blinked in the light. 'I prefer the gloom,' he said. He stretched and headed for the door. 'If you want me, I'll be with the accordion player.'

Finch paid no notice to his exit. She patted her hands and glared at the books as if they'd offended her. 'Couldn't we just say we looked?' she said. 'I want to do sword practice.'

Bert could see that she wasn't happy about reading. Ever since their brief time at school together, he'd had the impression that study was one of her least favourite activities. 'Aren't you even a little curious about what's happening to me?' he said.

'Fine,' said Finch grumpily. She took out a handful of titles and sat on the floor. Bert did the same. But it quickly became clear that finding the right information wouldn't be easy.

'There's just so much useless nonsense,' whined Finch.

Bert nodded. His initial excitement was damped by the musty old pages filled with descriptions of ancient court rituals and people with odd-sounding names. But eventually he managed to find some details about mage powers and how they manifested. He read on, trying to find his symptoms in the description. But the more he saw, the more his hopes sank.

Finch peered over his shoulder. 'What does it say?'

Bert frowned. 'I don't understand it,' he said. 'I've read through all the types of mage it has in this stupid book and there's nothing that sounds like me. There's no mention of blasts of power coming out of people's palms or any of the things I've been feeling.' He put his head in his hands. 'What if this is all just some terrible accident and the mirror at the museum really was just broken?'

'Let me see,' said Finch. She ran her finger over the different titles: 'Fire mages, mind mages, rock mages, metal mages . . .' She scratched her head. 'This all sounds like nonsense.'

Bert pushed away the books in disappointment.

'It's not surprising really,' said Finch. 'These are all books written by people from Penvellyn. There isn't much real writing from Ferenor left, and it seems like it's kept secret. But there are one or two people that have studied the old ways. They might have some answers.'

'You mean like Voss?' said Bert, glumly.

'I suppose,' said Finch. 'But there are friendly people too, like Hermatrude who lives out in the grand forest of Ferenor. She knows all about this kind of thing.'

Bert felt a little better, but he was beginning to worry about the spirit that he had seen. He couldn't deny that it had helped him, but what did it want? Voss had talked about it like it was a bundle of energy, and the doctor had said it could alter people's minds. But they both seemed convinced that it would try to contact him. The fact that it hadn't was unnerving. To make matters worse, the books said that if a spirit stayed in our world too long, it became dangerous.

That didn't sound particularly reassuring.

'I just wish I understood what was happening,' said Bert. 'I've got you and your dad into so much trouble already. I don't want to be a liability.'

Finch looked thoughtful. 'You know, my dad has been different since we've been helping you.' She paused. 'For the first time in a while he seems more like his old self.'

Bert was surprised. He could tell that Finch wanted to tell him something.

She looked at her metal feet. 'There was an accident, two years ago,' she said. 'An explosion in the hold. We still don't know what caused it. My mum was killed. I lost my legs.'

'I'm sorry,' said Bert.

Finch was quiet for a while. 'We always take risks,' she said. 'I just want to see him get excited about things again, like when we were off looking for treasure.' She seemed distant, as if she was deep in some memory. 'There's really nothing like treasure, Bert.'

Bert wanted to comfort her. Even though thoughts of treasure were far from his mind, he knew he should show interest. 'Are we likely to find any treasure?'

Finch smiled. 'I don't know whether you will,' she said tauntingly. 'But I think I've got a pretty good chance. And you'd better hope it's good, because we've done a lot of work for free already.' She seemed to cast away her misery, and helped him to his feet. But Bert detected a lingering sadness about her. 'Come on,' she said. 'Let's get some fresh air.'

Bert followed Finch out on to the deck. The sky was clear and the airship rocked gently in the breeze. Beneath their feet, the amphor engine rumbled, pumping warm air over the planks and keeping them powering towards Ferenor.

'I could get used to it here,' said Norton.

He was lying on the side of the hull, while an aeronaut played an accordion nearby. It was a sad song, about someone's death. It seemed to appeal to Norton's miserable tastes.

Bert smiled. 'You look like a regular pirate,' he said.

He was pleasantly surprised with how easily Norton took to airship life, but he still felt guilty for getting him involved. 'Is there anyone that's going to miss you, Norton?' he said. 'You never talked about your family.'

Norton shook his head. 'Not really my thing.'

Bert wasn't sure that answered his question.

'What are you doing daydreaming over there?' called Finch from across the deck. She was holding a pair of duelling sticks and tossed one of them to Bert.

Bert caught it clumsily. 'Is this really necessary?' he said. 'I mean, we only have a few hours. How much can I really learn about fighting that I don't already know?'

'Would you rather just sit around?' said Finch.

'It's a good place to do it,' said Norton.

'I just escaped from prison,' said Bert.

Finch didn't appear to be listening. She stepped in and swung at Bert's head. The sticks met with a sharp thwack. For the next few minutes they focused on the duel.

'Could we slow down a bit?' said Bert.

'This *is* me slowed down,' said Finch.

Norton let out a long yawn.

Bert winced and blocked another sharp swing.

After they'd trained for a while she finally relented and let him get a drink. They walked together to the front of the ship and looked over the blue horizon. Finch seemed pleased. 'You know, you're not bad at the basics,' she said.

'You just need confidence.'

'How do I get that?' asked Bert.

'You just do,' said Finch . 'You've got to control your feelings when you fight. It's not enough to be frightened, or angry. You have to have an idea of how you want to feel.'

Bert considered her words. 'What kind of dangers are you expecting?'

'I don't know exactly,' said Finch. 'Whenever you're in Ferenor, you're in wild country. There are creatures there that you won't find anywhere else in the world. Natural hazards too. And, of course, the possibility of finding some unstable artefact that still has magic power in it. But mostly you have to watch out for other people – scavengers and pirates, like us.'

'Why did you become pirates?' said Bert.

'My father didn't have a choice,' said Finch. 'He was a legitimate explorer once. But then the government outlawed non-government exploration of Ferenor. He either had to give up everything, or break the law.' She shrugged. 'It was no choice at all really. And of course, that meant there's never really been a choice for me either. Not that I'd change anything.'

'What's the island actually like?'

Finch looked distant. 'It's wonderful,' she said. 'There are these stretches of nothing – just wild land. And then you'll come across a ruin, and you'll see all these empty buildings, and monuments, and you get a sense of what it would have been like, when it was alive. But you won't find anything like Penvellyn City there. It was an older kind of living – full of warriors and mysticism. I suppose the best way I can describe it is like you're stepping back in time.'

Bert felt like he knew what she meant. It was the same kind of excitement he had felt reading stories about Ferenor as a child. The sense of reaching into the past.

'Is that why your father called the ship *Lugalbanda*?' he said.

Finch looked confused.

'Like the old myth,' said Bert, trying not to sound like he was showing off. 'A castle floating above the clouds. How the ancient people used to explain lightning.'

'Oh, right,' said Finch. 'I suppose so.' She scratched her head and twirled the fighting stick in her hand. 'Maybe he's right about me not reading enough of those books.'

Bert left Finch to her duties and rested for a while with Norton at the edge of the deck. The hours rolled by to the sound of the waves and the rumbling engine. The crewmen yelled to one another and hurried about their work. There were about two dozen of them, as far as Bert could tell. They were a brightly dressed bunch, with feathers in their flight caps and patterned scarfs – old and young, from all over the world. They seemed completely different from the professional soldiers back in Penvellyn, and nothing like Voss's men. But as he watched, Bert became aware of their tense expressions and their backward glances. It occurred to him that they were looking out for pursuers. He felt a shudder as he thought of Prince Voss and his state-of-the-art airship.

'Land ho!' called one of the crewmen from the rigging.

Bert looked up in surprise. He hadn't realized how much time had passed. A band of black lay on the horizon. He could feel the wind rising and saw grey clouds towering ahead.

The Professor stepped out on deck. 'Sooner than I expected,' he said. He turned to Finch. 'You'd better get Bert some cold-weather clothing and a weapon. We'll probably only get one pass at the Sethera Mountains.' He looked at the clouds. 'And it might get a little bumpy.'

Chapter 13

F inch took Bert to a small cabin under the hatchway and passed him some winter clothes and a new blade. 'Head back on deck when you're ready,' she said. 'And don't take long.'

'I won't,' said Bert.

He pulled on the thick padded jacket over his regular attire – his old school trousers, and the woollen jumper that the Professor had given him when he'd come aboard – and looked at himself in the reflection of a steam pipe. He couldn't help feeling proud. He'd only been on board the *Lugalbanda* for a day and already he was going on his first adventure. He had almost finished attaching his sword belt when he heard someone moving by the door.

'Who's there?' he said.

Norton stepped into view. 'Hello,' he said.

'What's going on?' asked Bert.

'Nothing,' said Norton. 'Just thinking.'

'About what?'

'Well, you know, life.'

Bert could tell that Norton was unhappy, but he was too occupied by his preparations to give it much consideration. He finished fastening his belt.

'Bert,' said Norton.

'What?' said Bert, checking his reflection again.

'I don't think you should go down to that wreck.'

Bert frowned in surprise. '*What?*'

Norton spoke hurriedly. 'I mean, you can tell the whole thing is going to be miserable,' he said. 'You've got to get down there to start with, and that looks dangerous enough. And that wreck is probably all musty and cold. And there might be, you know, diseases.' He looked at his feet, as if he was struggling to find the right words. 'It's just not really our kind of thing.'

Bert was too annoyed to reply. He couldn't understand why Norton would bring this up now. He felt like his friend was trying to ruin his confidence when he needed it most.

'So?' said Norton.

'So what?' said Bert.

'Will you stay here?'

Bert fastened up his jacket angrily. 'I need to do this,' he said. 'You don't understand. I'm sorry you ended up with us, but if you're not going to help, just leave me alone.'

Norton looked hurt. 'You don't want me here?'

'I didn't mean that,' said Bert. 'I just mean . . . you know.'

'Were you going to leave me in Penvellyn?'

Bert was becoming flustered. 'Look, Norton,' he said. 'There are more things to this world than sitting around and reading poetry. Sometimes you have to make quick choices.'

'You weren't even going to say goodbye?' said Norton.

Bert sighed. The guiltier he felt, the more frustrated he became. 'Why are we even talking about this? I'm trying to do something important. You're just getting in the way.'

An angry silence fell between them.

Norton sighed. 'I'm not saying this is easy,' he said. 'I'm just saying, maybe you shouldn't rush into something dangerous. Maybe try waiting to see if the spirit has a plan?'

Bert scoffed and shook his head. 'That spirit has been trouble from the beginning,' he said. 'The sooner I find a cure for all this, and get rid of it for good, the better.'

Norton gave Bert a pained look – something deeper than his usual sadness. He nodded and looked down at his feet, and then shuffled out of the room.

Bert looked at his reflection. His face was flushed with anger and his eyes were watering. He shook his head and rushed after Norton. 'Hang on,' he called.

When he reached the gangway there was no one there. Norton had vanished. He sighed and paced back to the cabin. 'What's got into him?' he muttered.

His hands shook as he fastened his buttons. He knew he shouldn't have lost his temper. Norton was only looking out for him, even if he was doing it in an annoying way. He sighed. He knew Finch would be getting impatient. The ship shook in the force of the wind. There was no time to catch up with Norton now. He gave one last look at his reflection, no longer feeling proud of himself and his new clothes, and headed to the deck hatch.

When he stepped out on deck they were almost at the mountains. Below them lay the land of Ferenor. It didn't look especially magical. Aside from the looming peaks ahead, he could only see a mass of dark forests and brown rivers. There weren't even any birds. The hull rocked and the gasbag creaked. The Professor yelled orders to the man at the ship's controls. Meanwhile, Finch was eating some chocolate. 'Do you want a piece?' she said, offering him the packet.

'No thanks,' said Bert. Even through the thick clothes Finch had given him he could feel the chill. He began to sense why people were wary of this place.

'Nervous?' said Finch.

Bert shook his head. He was still thinking about what Norton had said, and feeling guilty. He wished his friend would appear on deck so he could apologize.

'There it is – the wreck of the *Erebus*,' yelled the Professor. He pointed over the side of the hull to a small dark shape that was sticking out of the snow of one of the nearby mountain tops. 'It looks fairly intact.'

Bert squinted at the shape. As they drew closer he could make out the rear of a ship. It was mostly buried in the ice and snow. There were black rocks all around.

'All right, get ready,' said Finch.

Bert nodded. The excitement was building now. He shook away his other thoughts. The idea of making a foolish mistake scared him almost as much as any physical danger.

The *Lugalbanda* battled its way down through the crosswinds and floated beside the wreck. The engine rattled. It was clear that they wouldn't be able to hover for long.

'Look after the ship, Peel,' said the Professor. 'You should go to the sheltered side of the mountain until we signal. If you need to alert us, fire the guns.'

Peel nodded and tapped his nose.

Bert realized that it was just him, the Professor and Finch that were going to land. 'How will we get down there?' he yelled over the sound of the engine. There was the height of a house between the deck and the mountainside, and the wind was too strong for rope ladders.

'Let's see,' said the Professor. He tossed a sack overboard and watched it sink into the white blanket beneath them. 'Ah yes, that's perfect,' he said. Without any further explanation, he clambered over the hull and jumped off, plunging into the snow.

Finch climbed over too. 'Come on, Bert!'

Bert clung to the side of the hull and looked down. The wind was biting and the sound of the engine rattled through his head. He closed his eyes and leapt.

His stomach lurched and his ears whistled, then he felt a soft thump as the snow hit his back. In another moment the Professor emerged beside him, grinning through a mask of white powder. 'Better than swinging on a rope in these winds,' he explained.

They grouped together and headed straight for the wreck. The cold was biting, even through Bert's heavy layers of clothing, and each footstep sank deep into the drifts.

The Professor stopped before they reached the visible part of the wreck and began excavating. He tossed Bert and

Finch a pickaxe each and pointed for them to dig too.

They quickly made a burrow through the top layer of the ice and passed into more crumbly snow. After a short time, the Professor struck something hollow. He reached into the ice chippings, searched for a moment, and then heaved open a large wooden hatch. 'One of the lower deck entrances,' he explained. 'Right where I thought it would be, of course.'

'You can boast when we get out of the cold,' said Finch. 'My joints are seizing.' She swung herself down through the hatch and disappeared into the darkness.

'After you, Bert,' said the Professor.

Bert shuffled forwards and followed the rungs of a ladder down until his feet touched a strangely slanted floor. The Professor and Finch lit their amphor safety lanterns to reveal a large open space inside the airship. A row of tables and chairs lay piled against the lower wall.

'We're in the galley,' said Bert. He noticed food on the plates that lay scattered over the boards. 'They can't have had much warning before they crashed.'

'Or they hated washing up as much as we do,' said the Professor.

'No, Bert's right,' said Finch. She pointed her lantern at a dead body by Bert's shoulder. It was frozen in a seated position, still holding a knife and fork.

Bert flinched away. 'Thanks for that, Finch,' he said.

Finch smirked and gave a mock salute.

'All right you two, follow me,' said the Professor.

They grouped together again and began making their way slowly through the dark wreckage of the *Erebus*. The ice creaked above them, and the wind moaned. Bert tried to focus on the Professor's footsteps. It seemed like he was looking for something in particular.

'This way,' he said, gesturing to a doorway.

The light of the lantern revealed a narrow gangway that sloped upwards. The boards had ruptured, and piles of snow blocked their way.

As they knocked aside the last ice barrier Bert thought he saw something moving. He raised his hand to point it out, but by then it had disappeared.

'What's wrong?' said the Professor, reaching for his sword.

'At the top of the slope,' said Bert. 'I thought I saw someone.'

The Professor let go of his sword hilt and shook his head. 'It'll be another dead body, Bert. Or our own shadows. There's no way anyone survived in here.'

Finch poked Bert in the ribs. 'Unless it's a ghost?'

'That's not funny,' said Bert. A shiver ran down his spine. He watched the corner where he'd seen the movement as they continued their ascent.

At the top they came to a closed doorway.

'We should be getting close,' said the Professor. He knocked ice away from the hinges with his pick, took a run-up and barged the door open.

Inside was a much larger room, lined with shelves and stacks of barrels. Thick beams crossed the ceiling, and the air smelt faintly of vinegar.

'Interesting,' said the Professor. 'We appear to be in the storage hold.'

'The ship must have been huge,' said Finch. 'Look at all the gunpowder.' She nudged a barrel with her foot as she passed, revealing the warning symbol for explosives.

'Wonderful,' muttered Bert. He pulled his collar higher and squinted into the darkness. He felt like they were being watched. He'd hated ghost stories ever since he could remember. As they passed by the dark rows of shelves his teeth began to chatter.

'Are you scared, Bert?' said Finch.

'Just cold,' said Bert. 'Maybe we should move faster?'

The Professor laughed. 'He's been spending too much time with you, Finch. Your impatience has rubbed off on him.' He made his way forwards and opened the door to the next room. 'The captain's cabin,' he said. He stepped aside to allow Bert and Finch to enter.

The room was colder than the rest of the ship. A row of icicles hung from the ceiling and a frozen figure sat hunched over a large desk. The Professor mimed tipping his hat, and said: 'Permission to come aboard, Captain?'

'Did you know him?' asked Bert.

'Mostly by reputation,' said the Professor. 'Anyway, I'm afraid we don't have time for reminiscences. We need to plunder this logbook and see if we can gain any clues on the mirror.' He moved the body of the captain aside and began to search the desk.

'Where would it be?' said Bert.

'I think I've already found it,' said the Professor, pointing to a safe under the table. He took some tools from his pockets. 'It might take me a few moments to crack this thing open. You two can explore if you want, but don't go too far.'

'Understood,' said Finch. She headed back to the storage hold.

Bert followed, but he couldn't escape the sense that something sinister was close at hand. As Finch cast the light of her lantern around the room he noticed strange marks in the walls and shelves, and splintered wood on the floor. 'Have you seen this, Finch?' he said.

'What?'

'It looks like the place was smashed up from the inside.'

Finch squinted at the marks. 'I was hoping you'd found treasure,' she said. 'But you're right. These are sword strikes.' She lifted her lantern high and surveyed the rest of the room.

'It looks like there was a battle in here,' said Bert. 'Do you think that could be part of why they crashed? Maybe they were attacked?'

'With the captain sitting calmly in his cabin, and people eating in the galley?' said Finch. 'And anyway, if there was a fight here, where are the bodies?'

Bert didn't like the impression the clues were making on him. He began to suspect something unnatural had happened to the ship – something very sudden.

There was a thump at the door that made both of them jump, and the Professor reappeared. He passed a thick book to Bert with a smile. 'The records we need are inside, just as we thought,' he said, clapping his hands. 'I'm going to search the rest of the captain's cabin. You can have a look around too, Bert – see if anything catches your attention.' He headed back into the room.

Bert looked at Finch for reassurance.

'You go on,' she said. 'I'm just going to search their supplies a little, and then I'll come through and join you. I thought I saw a brace of pistols lying around.'

'All right,' said Bert. He followed the Professor into the cabin and flicked through the pages of the logbook as he went. It occurred to him that he should read the final entries to find out what had happened to the ship. They were made up of a series of hastily scribbled notes. He was about to turn a page when something caught his attention: '*The young Prince Voss...*'

He paused and read it over again:

The young Prince Voss seemed pleased with the last delivery. I have to say, I was surprised by the depth of his knowledge of Ferenor history, although I hope his enthusiasm does not lead him to tamper with things beyond his control. He appears to have read every text I have encountered on the subject of magic in the old times, and a great many that I have not ...

Bert frowned. It was unnerving to find a famous adventurer like Amleth writing about Prince Voss in friendly terms. It also made it harder to dismiss the prince as a madman.

He gave me an artefact from the royal collection that I have not heard of before – a 'ward stone' apparently made by the necromancers of the north – that he claims will protect the ship from evil spirits. Of course, I doubt it is anything but junk, but I am proud to accept any gift from the royal line. Perhaps this means that the king will soon put his full support behind our expeditions, instead of insisting on this mad policy of magic suppression and denial ...

Bert skipped ahead a few pages. For now, he was more

concerned about what had happened to the ship than the shady politics of Penvellyn.

There have been difficulties. We have escaped the storm, but three crewmen are badly injured. Events were as follows. Aeronaut Appleby reported seeing the three crewmen heading into the storage hold to gather supplies. When they failed to reappear, he went to look for them and found them all lying unconscious around the 'ward stone' that Prince Voss gave me. It seems the object may have some dangerous powers after all. I blame myself for this blunder. The affected men are unconscious and in a serious condition. To make matters worse, a strange miasma seems to hang over the ship, and the light itself seems dull and foetid.

There was a gap denoting some unspecified passage of time.

Horrible events. The surgeon reports that the ill crewmen died – then suddenly rose up, and began to attack people around them. The crew managed to restrain one of them but two others are at large somewhere in the lower deck. They seem to be averse to light, and as such are probably hiding in the ventilation pipes. My men are currently investigating. Surgeon Wakes, who was bitten by one of the risen, has subsequently fallen into the same catatonic state.

'Professor?' said Bert. 'You should probably read this.'

'What?'

'There's an account of the crash.'

'Oh, very good, Bert,' said the Professor. 'I just need a moment to pry open this chest. I have a feeling if there were anything else of value, it would be in here . . .'

Bert looked back towards the doorway, but there was no sound from Finch – only the moaning of the wind outside. He took a deep breath and continued to read.

The situation is dire. Half of the crew have succumbed to the illness or been killed. There was a sudden attack by the creatures – having seen the risen men up close for myself, I can attest that they are no longer human – during the Second Watch's evening meal. More of the afflicted are rising even as I write. I am turning the ship off course to make an emergency landing as soon as we clear the forest, where we will destroy the vessel and set out with what supplies we can. It is a desperate plan, but in my opinion it is the only course left to us. I curse my foolishness for accepting that terrible object from the Prince. Where could he have found such a thing, and why would he have given it to us? I must confront him if I survive this ordeal . . .

There was a final chilling entry.

All is lost. The crew has been overcome. I am the last man left, and I am now trapped in my cabin. A strange, black liquid covers the walls. It seems to drain my energy, and prevents me from breaking through the planks. The air is stifling. Under the circumstances, I feel assured that the ship will soon crash – I only wish that I could make sure of its total destruction. I leave this as a record of what has occurred, and a warning to any others that reach this ship – the crew may be dead, but they do not rest, and I fear they never will. Get away as fast as you can.

Bert's breath seemed to leave his body. 'Professor, you have to read this right now,' he said. He forced the book under the Professor's nose, and pointed to the last section.

The Professor read it swiftly. 'Oh,' he said. 'That isn't good.'

Just then Bert noticed something above them, and cast the light of the Professor's lantern upwards. It revealed two words carved in large letters on the ceiling:

'GET AWAY'.

Chapter 14

....

Bert and the Professor stared at the stark warning scrawled across the ceiling. Bert hardly dared move.

'Hmmm,' said the Professor. He raised his voice: 'Finch!'

Finch gave a yell of alarm from the storage hold. She rushed to the doorway and called them over with a wave of her hand. 'Look at that thing,' she said.

Something was shambling out of the gloom. To begin with Bert only saw a mass of rags in the darkness. But as it came closer he saw a bony leg and a grinning skull.

'What is it?' said Bert.

'It seems to be a living skeleton,' said the Professor, in obvious puzzlement.

The skeleton walked jerkily towards them.

'It seems pretty harmless,' said Finch.

The skeleton gave a sudden scream and charged at her.

The Professor cut it short with a swift punch. The blow hit with a force that sent the grey bones shattering to pieces. 'It's not harmless,' he said. 'What happened?'

'I just opened a cupboard and that thing came out,' said Finch. She looked more annoyed than shaken. 'That's not that spirit you were talking about, is it Bert?'

Bert shook his head. 'My spirit didn't look like that.'

'Well, we've got what we needed,' said the Professor. 'It's probably time we left.' As he spoke there was a crunch in the ice overhead, and a skeletal hand appeared through the ceiling.

Bert gave a cry of surprise.

'Get out of here, you two,' said the Professor. He snapped the arm in two with a quick swipe. 'We'll make our way back to the airship and burn this place behind us.'

'I'll check the way out,' said Bert. He hurried ahead to the door but found that it was shut fast. He was sure that they had left it open when they entered.

The Professor drew his sword and stood facing a shuddering block of ice against the far wall. Something seemed to be trying to force its way through.

'How's that exit, Bert?' said Finch, catching up to him.

Bert shoved his shoulder against the door but it wouldn't budge. He tried again but it felt like someone was pressing on it from the other side. He looked around and saw black liquid running down the walls, pooling in every corner of the room. 'I can't get out,' he gasped.

Finch ran up and kicked the door. It made a cracking sound but didn't budge. 'There's something holding it closed,' she said. 'Draw your sword.'

Bert reached down and fumbled for the hilt.

'Just like training,' said Finch, reassuringly. 'Don't get panicked.'

Bert drew his sword calmly and nodded.

The light from the lanterns grew dull and began to stutter, and the closeness of the air made him feel ill. Something powerful was approaching. There wasn't a way out. It felt more like they were in a dark cave than the hold of a ship.

Suddenly, a large grey skeleton stepped from the door of a nearby locker, moving as casually if it was walking out of one room and into another. It had a large sword in its hand and was covered in old, rusted armour. It swung an upwards blow at the Professor, then reversed the blade's momentum and delivered a mighty chop downwards, aiming for his head.

The Professor dodged aside and knocked the blade away. He cracked the figure's chest with a flash of his sword and then braced his legs and punched from his shoulder. There was a snap like breaking wood, and the skeleton disintegrated across the planks.

'I don't like the look of these things,' said the Professor.

'Well, at least they're not invincible,' said Finch. She ran to a ruptured section of the wall and tried kicking the planks. The hull shook, and a pile of snow burst in. 'We might be able to get out this way,' she said. 'Hold them off for a moment while I try and make a tunnel.'

Bert nodded, but as he stood guard another shambling figure stepped into view, then another, and another. A whole host of skeletons were emerging from hiding.

'Keep your guard up,' yelled the Professor. He ran forward and drew out two of the skeletons with a series of attacks, but a third raced past and made for Bert. His instincts kicked in as the skeleton charged. He raised his hand and a shockwave blasted the creature to pieces.

Another skeleton dropped down from the beams.

He barely had time to block its sword. The blow was strong, but he caught it squarely and forced the sharp end downwards, like he'd been taught in training.

He lashed out with his own attack.

His sword seemed to pass straight through the skeleton's ribs. The creature made a hissing sound, and swung again. It was only by a lucky dodge that he avoided the blade.

'Don't let them corner you!' yelled the Professor.

Bert raised his guard again and tried to focus but a feeling of helplessness came over him. The creature was fast and nimble and his first attack hadn't hurt it at all.

The skeleton drew its sword high and swung at his head.

Finch leapt in and took the skeleton's head off with a swift kick. 'There's too many of them to try digging our way out,' she said. 'Try to keep dodging.' She spun to a metal crate as she spoke, and kicked with the full force of her metal leg. There was a sharp clang and the crate shot across the floor, knocking the legs from under a group of skeletons.

Bert was separated from her as another attacker ran in. He blocked deftly but he winced at the speed of the creature's strike. It wasn't giving him a chance to use his powers.

The skeleton gave a hiss, grabbed his sword, and knocked him back. The weapon sprang from his grasp. He thudded against a stack of barrels and felt the air leave his lungs.

The skeleton swung at his head.

He ducked just in time and raised his hand. There was a sharp flash and the creature's bones fell to fragments. He breathed a sigh of relief and snatched his sword from the floor.

When he turned, he was horrified to find even more of

the creatures had invaded the hold. Finch was kicking skeletons left and right. Their bones went rattling along the floor.

Bert couldn't even see the Professor clearly any more, only white flashes and dark blades where he was fighting at the other side of the shelves. Bert ran to help but as he did so another creature appeared in front of him. This one held an axe. It swung broadly and shattered the crates on either side of Bert's head. The splinters spun in the air and stung his face.

He pointed his hand at it and tried to will the power to strike. But this time nothing happened. A pain shot through his palm and he felt coldness around his heart. It occurred to him that he had never used his power this frequently. He felt suddenly weak.

The axe came in again. This time Bert got his sword up to block but the blow was too strong. His weapon sprang out of his hands again with a sharp clank and spun across the floor. He staggered up on to the crates, climbing frantically as the axe chopped down. A stack of barrels exploded behind him as he ran. The axe became embedded in the hull and the skeleton snarled.

As Bert was struggling to get away he saw a pair of skeletons charging for Finch. He could see that she was already engaged in a duel with a fierce-looking creature.

He leapt from the boxes and tackled them.

The skeletons fell with him and they landed in a heap amongst a pile of ropes. One of the creatures grabbed his arm and wouldn't let go. The other grabbed his feet.

The axe-wielding skeleton was approaching.

Bert felt a jolt of fear. 'Help!' he yelled.

Finch leapt high across the hold and swung from a beam to land beside Bert. She kicked one skeleton to pieces and struck the other's arm off. 'Keep fighting,' she said.

Bert leapt to his feet and managed a quick 'Thanks' before the axe-wielding skeleton charged.

'Look out!' shouted Bert. He pulled Finch aside and raised his hand. A shockwave blasted a thick cloud of dust around him and took the creature off its feet, and a sharp pain shot through Bert's chest. He clutched his hand. One of the lanterns cracked and a lick of flame shot across the floor.

'What's wrong?' asked Finch.

'I'm all right,' said Bert, shaking away the pain.

'Try your power on the door,' yelled the Professor. 'Don't hit the explosives.'

Bert shuddered when he remembered the barrels of gunpowder lying around. Finch was already fighting another sword-wielding skeleton. 'I'll keep you covered,' she called over her shoulder.

Bert nodded. He opened his palm and put his hand

against the door. Nothing happened. A thick black tar covered the woodwork and made a sucking sound against his skin. The scar's energy seemed to fade from his body. He snatched his hand back and tried again.

This time it felt even weaker. 'Come on,' he urged.

A host of creatures were converging on them. The Professor was firing off punches and swings in every direction and somehow dodging the incoming blows, but he was surrounded by enemies. There was no way he could reach them in time.

Finch was struggling to keep the monsters back.

Bert closed his eyes and tried to focus. He raised his palm and aimed at the door, trying to feel the energy. He could see the glow crackling around his scar.

Something blunt hit his shoulder and sent him tumbling.

'Bert!' yelled Finch. She helped him up and kicked apart the skeleton that had attacked him, but the rest of the creatures were quick to follow. They backed them into a corner.

'Keep close,' said Finch.

Bert felt dizzy from the blow. He saw a line of skulls peering at him in the glow of the flames from the broken lantern. It was like a nightmare.

Suddenly he saw smoke in front of him. It seemed to rise from his skin, growing thicker and more distinct, until a grey figure appeared, floating over the ground.

Bert blinked in shock. 'The spirit,' he said. 'The spirit from the prison.'

The skeletons raised their weapons and slunk back from the new apparition. They were clearly afraid of it. Their jaws hung open in almost comical surprise.

The Professor glanced around. 'What's got into them?'

'Can't you see it?' said Bert.

The apparition raised its hands and a burst of red light swept over the room. The light passed harmlessly over Bert, Finch and the Professor, but it hit the skeletons like an explosion. With a piercing scream the creatures fell into dust. Bert sensed that the spirit had used all of its energy in the attack. It seemed to shimmer in his vision, grow more solid, and sink to the floor.

Bert was stunned for a moment. He couldn't see clearly, but he could still hear the flames of the lantern licking against the wall and crackling along the beams. The ice was melting fast and a thick, hissing steam rolled across the room. In the spot where the spirit had fallen, he saw a small dark shape lying on the planks. It looked like a person.

He hurried over to it. 'Hey,' he said.

The Professor and Finch met in the centre of the room and looked at Bert in confusion. 'What are you staring at?' said Finch. 'What was that light?'

'I think someone's hurt here,' said Bert.

There was rumble of distant cannon fire.

'That's the warning shot,' said the Professor. 'We'd better get back to the ship. We can thank our stars about this later,' he said, grabbing Bert's shoulder.

'Wait!' repeated Bert. He knelt over the figure.

'What are you looking at?' said Finch.

Bert was annoyed by their obliviousness. It was as if they couldn't see the person at all. He leant down and turned the figure over. For a moment he was stunned.

'Norton?' he said.

Norton blinked up at him. 'Hello, Bert.'

There was a thump above them, and a deep rumble. The Professor looked alarmed. 'I don't like that,' he said. 'Come on, Bert. This isn't a good time to become dead weight.'

'Wait,' said Finch. 'I think he can see something.'

Bert was too stunned to think clearly. 'Norton,' he said. 'What on earth are you doing here? You were supposed to stay on the ship. Why would you have followed us?'

The Professor and Finch stared at him in apparent concern.

'Did you hit your head, Bert?' asked Finch.

'It's Norton,' said Bert. He couldn't understand why they were being so dense. 'We've got to get him out of here. Somehow he must have got down from the ship.'

'Who's Norton?' said the Professor.

Bert stared at him. 'Norton, my friend,' said Bert. He felt like he was trapped in a bad dream. 'He's been my friend since . . . since . . .' He found himself growing confused. He realized that he couldn't remember having seen Norton before the day at the museum. But another part of his mind told him that he had known Norton for years. It didn't make sense. He was getting dizzy.

There was a sudden thump close by and the door burst open. A group of soldiers flooded the hold with their guns raised and a small shiny object flashed over the floor. Bert flinched away from it on instinct and recognized the dark crystal from the prison.

'Look out!' shouted the Professor.

Norton reached out his hand to Bert. He opened his mouth as if to say something, but no sound came out. The crystal ignited beside him with its eerie green glow.

Norton's grip passed through Bert's fingers.

'Norton!' yelled Bert. He clutched for his friend's hand but there was nothing to get hold of. It was as if he was swiping through smoke. 'What's happening?'

Norton's face had almost vanished.

Bert resisted the pain and made a grab for the crystal, but by then it was too late. The green light crackled and went out, and Norton was gone. It was as if he had never been there at all.

Chapter 15

Heavy footsteps crunched over the wreckage of the hold floor. Voss stepped out from behind the soldiers. 'I wouldn't advise trying to run,' he said. 'My men are good shots.'

The Professor and Finch looked at him warily.

Bert had a hollow feeling in his chest. He looked down at his hand and felt a sharp pain. Through his bandages he could see his skin turning a purple tinge.

Voss approached. 'I suppose you might experience some side effects, being severed from your spirit friend like that.' He picked up the dark crystal and placed it into a small, spherical frame, surrounded by glass. 'I have it contained now. Whatever happens to you will make no difference to my plans. I no longer need your power to keep it alive.'

Bert felt suddenly weak. His head swam.

Voss held up the glowing sphere and paced back over the room. 'You should have been more cooperative, boy,' he said. 'I might have let you live.' He picked up the logbook.

Finch leant forward on her feet.

'I wouldn't,' said Voss.

The Professor nodded and Finch relented. The soldiers had them covered, but Bert could sense that they were eyeing the room – looking for some way out.

Voss tossed the logbook into the flames and watched it burn. 'There are no answers for you here,' he said. 'A person like you was never meant for power.'

Bert tried to stand. His thoughts grew clearer. He knew now that the person he'd thought of as Norton had been the spirit all along. He couldn't let Voss take his friend away. A sense of desperation took hold. He could already feel the pain of the spirit being drawn away from him. 'Give him back to me,' he said. 'You don't know what you're doing.'

'I know exactly what I'm doing,' snapped Voss. His words echoed in the small space. The hold fell silent except for the crackling flames. Voss walked back to the soldiers.

'I have information,' said the Professor. 'Something important.'

Voss hesitated. He paused by the row of guns. 'I can see that you're just trying to delay the inevitable. I thought that a man like you would know when he's beaten.'

'It could save your life,' said the Professor.

Voss looked at him levelly. 'Tell me what you know, pirate, and I might let your daughter choose prison instead of death,' he said.

The Professor nodded seriously. 'All right,' he said. 'It's actually better that I tell you sooner rather than later. You see, those flames have reached the explosives.'

Voss flinched and looked at the flames.

The soldiers wavered in their aim.

The Professor grabbed Finch and Bert and dived behind a row of crates. There was a ripple of gunshots. The bullets crackled by and drove into the planks around them.

'Don't let them escape,' yelled Voss. He was already moving for the door, leaving the soldiers to hesitate between doing their duty and preserving their lives.

Finch pointed to the hole in the wall that she'd made during the fight. There was already the beginning of a burrow in the snow. 'I can break through there,' she said.

A soldier fired another shot at them. The bullet snapped into the planks.

'Wait for the right moment,' said the Professor.

Bert put a hand against the floor to steady himself. He felt terrible. The Professor placed an arm around his shoulders and they crouched together, ready to spring.

'Come out!' ordered a soldier.

'You should give up,' shouted the Professor. 'You'll get us all killed.'

'The bloodline guards do not fear death,' yelled the soldier.

'Great,' muttered the Professor. 'That's just what we need.'

The flames grew louder and began to hiss.

A bullet cracked off the surface of the box beside Bert's head and he flinched away. The soldiers were clearly intent on fulfilling their duty, whatever the cost.

The smoke in the room grew thicker.

'Well, we've got to go for it,' said the Professor. He gripped Bert tighter and prepared to run. They all knew the risk. It was unlikely the soldiers would miss again.

'My count,' said Finch. 'Three . . . Two . . .'

There was a yelp of pain from across the room followed by a heavy thud.

A gunshot rang out and crunched off the ceiling. Blades clashed and there was the sound of a struggle.

'Traitor!' yelled a startled voice. Another thump followed.

Bert peeked over the crates.

A man in a black coat threw one of the soldiers against the wall. A sword appeared in his hand and he went to attack the next man. There was a cry of pain. Three soldiers swung their guns towards the attacker but he seemed to strike them all down in a blur. For a moment Bert felt he was dreaming. His mind flashed to his earliest memories – the man in the hooded cloak, coming to save him once again. He coughed and shook his head in confusion.

The man sprinted over to them and revealed his face. '*Cassius?*' Bert gasped. He felt a wave of unease. 'What on earth are you doing here?'

The quæstor put his hand on Bert's shoulder. 'Are you hurt?' he said.

The Professor frowned. 'What answer are you hoping for?'

'I'm here to help,' said Cassius. 'I'll explain later.'

Just then the smoke rippled across the ceiling and a torrent of flame shot upwards. The fire from the lantern had spread over both walls. Cassius moved in a blur, throwing Bert and Finch towards the Professor. 'Get out,' he yelled. The whole of the hold seemed to be taking flame. Bert struggled forward, coughing badly and huddling low to escape the heat.

He felt Finch's hand on his shoulder.

'This way,' she said. She sent a powerful kick into the ice then began digging with her pick. The others struggled through behind her. The snow closed in.

There was a sudden rush of air as they reached the surface.

'Keep running,' said the Professor.

Bert was weakening fast and the pain in his hand throbbed. But he focused on their voices and felt their hands pushing him along through the deep snow.

The ground fell away under his feet.

'Hold on,' said the Professor. He grabbed Bert and they plunged together; sliding down the ice, dropping through space, then crashing into a snowy hollow.

Bert caught a glimpse of a large grey airship floating above them. A group of soldiers were waving and yelling from the mountaintop. Apparently, they'd been left behind.

Bert felt a pang of pity for them.

A huge explosion split the air. Bert felt a snap like a rubber band inside his ear, and everything turned white. The next thing he was aware of was a strong pair of arms pulling him upwards as huge flurry of ice pattered down around them. When the smoke cleared the wreck of the *Erebus* was no more, and the soldiers had vanished. Bert heard Cassius and the Professor talking – arguing over something – but he wasn't paying attention. He was staring after Voss's ship as it faded far into the distance and thinking of his last conversation with Norton. A terrible sense of guilt welled up inside him. It was worse than any fear he felt for himself. His friend had tried to warn him about the wreck and he hadn't listened. Now it was too late. Norton was gone.

Bert was barely conscious as they carried him aboard the *Lugalbanda*. He was vaguely aware of Finch and the Professor talking to him, and of someone mopping his brow with cold water. But the rest was lost to strange dreams and the fierce pain in his arm. He kept seeing faces hovering over him. Sometimes he thought Norton was there. He kept trying to apologize.

A calm voice spoke to him. 'We're going to get you to help, Bert. There's a woman who lives out in the wastes of Ferenor – an excellent healer. Just hold on.'

He faded out of consciousness again and dreamt he was riding in a carriage. The swaying of the airship became the rocking of the wheels. His clothes were muddy. A man in a cloak sat beside him. He had been afraid, and the man had rescued him. He tried to remember further back. There were two people – a man and a woman. One of them ruffled his hair.

A shadow fell on him and cold air passed over his skin.

He felt as if he was ascending. Clouds hovered in his vision, almost in his grasp. Their peaks looked like castles. His feet set down on the nearest slope and he began to climb. He knew he needed to reach the top.

'Bert?' said Finch's voice. 'Bert, wake up.'

He opened his eyes and found himself in bed in an unfamiliar room. Daylight shone through an oval window. The ceiling looked as if it was made from packed earth, criss-crossed with wicker beams. It took him a while to shake away the feelings of his dream, but he quickly remembered the events of the airship and looked down at his hand. It was painful and discoloured.

'Norton,' he mumbled.

Finch was sitting beside him. 'I knew it,' she said. 'I told them you'd wake up.'

'Where are we?' said Bert.

'Hermatrude's house,' said Finch. 'She's sort of an aunty of mine. And she's an inventor, too. She's really clever, Bert. She'll know how to get you back to normal.'

'Are we still in Ferenor?' said Bert.

Finch nodded. 'Don't try to sit up,' she said. 'I'll go get her.' She hurried from the room and returned a moment later, leading a hunched, elderly lady by the hand.

The lady smiled as she examined Bert. 'You were in a bad way,' she said, kindly 'He was right to bring you to me. Though he should have brought you sooner.'

'You healed me?' asked Bert.

'I treated you,' said the woman. 'I'm afraid healing is beyond my skills. I heard what happened to you and your spirit.' She shook her head. 'It is a terrible thing.'

'But he'll be all right, won't he?' said Finch.

Hermatrude took out a bottle of medicine rather than reply.

Belt felt a pang of anger when he remembered what Voss had done. He clenched his fists and pushed aside the bedsheets. 'I have to save Norton,' he said. He tried to stand, but his vision blurred and his arms shook. He sank back against the pillows. 'I can feel it,' he said. 'The further he gets from me the worse I feel. It's like I'm running out of air.'

Hermatrude picked up a bucket of water and some bandages and inspected Bert's hand. He felt dizzy. Odd-looking plants hung in the window. The smell of herbs filled the room.

'That sounds like the spirit line,' she said.

'You know about magic?' asked Bert.

'I have learnt a little about it,' she said. 'Though less than you, I expect.' She washed his palm with a damp cloth and began to apply a new bandage. 'This mark is definitely part of a mage ritual,' she said. 'But as to whether it will fade, or grow more harmful, I can't truly say. I have given you some medicine to strengthen you through the ordeal – the rest is down to your constitution.'

Bert swallowed. He knew instinctively that there was no hope for him unless he reached Norton. He couldn't just wait around in bed, hoping to get better. He had to act.

'Are you all right?' asked Hermatrude.

'I need to get up,' he said.

'You need to rest,' said Hermatrude.

Bert was struggling to stay calm. 'They've taken away Norton . . . my spirit. I've let him down.' He shook his head in dismay. The grief was too much to put into words.

'It's all right, Bert,' said Finch. She squeezed his hand.

Hermatrude looked serious. 'The line between mages and their spirits is strong. I have often read about the power of the ritual. It has taken on a part of your soul, Bert. You almost died when you were separated. Now you must try to conserve your strength.'

Bert understood what she was saying, but in his heart he didn't care about mage rituals or magic powers, only that his friend had been taken. It made him feel hollow.

Hermatrude looked concerned and gave a sigh. 'I am going to tell the others that you are awake,' she said. 'Please, try not to exert yourself. You're already very weak.'

Bert stared at the patterns of wicker on the ceiling. He knew he needed to leave this place and pursue Voss. But it was hard to keep his eyes open.

'We should leave him,' said Hermatrude. 'And you should rest, too.'

'I can stay,' said Finch.

'No,' said Hermatrude. 'Come and eat something.'

Bert was vaguely aware of their footsteps leaving the room. He thought back to what Voss had said, about not needing his energy to keep Norton alive any more. He sensed that the prince was planning something terrible. He forced his eyes open and tried to sit up.

'I can't let him win,' he said. He looked down at his hand. The purple tinge seemed to pulse beneath his skin and the pain made his head swim. He clenched his fist. Inside he felt a cold power stirring. The energy strengthened him, even though it hurt.

He shifted his feet out of the bed and stood up. The shakiness passed after a moment, and the energy kept him standing. He clenched his fist harder and went to open the door.

He emerged in a burrow-like hallway filled with the scent of woodsmoke. He followed the smell to a half-open doorway. He could hear voices on the other side.

'Where does he think it is?' said the Professor.

Cassius spoke calmly. 'Tralvere. I managed to spy on some of his writings and studied the navigation room. Everything points to something above Tralvere.'

Bert was shocked to hear the quæstor's voice. He remembered the rescue from the airship but he still couldn't believe they were trusting the man who had chased them.

'That doesn't make any sense,' said the Professor. 'Tralvere is flatland, to the north. There's no high ground there for miles around. There aren't even any ruins.'

Bert pushed the door open.

The Professor and Cassius looked at him in surprise.

'You're awake?' said the Professor. 'You should be resting.'

Bert frowned at Cassius. 'What's he doing here?' he said.

'It's all right, Bert,' said the Professor. 'He's a friend.'

Bert frowned. He sensed some sort of trick.

'I'll explain,' said Cassius. 'But you should at least sit down.' He helped Bert into one of the seats beside the fireplace and threw another log on to the flames.

'He's the one who's been secretly helping us,' said the Professor. 'He sent us the message about getting you out of prison. He was trying to help you back in Penvellyn, too, though I'm afraid I didn't appreciate it at the time. I'm sorry about the knocks I gave you.'

'It's hardly worth mentioning,' said Cassius.

'I don't understand,' said Bert, sitting shakily.

'I've been tasked by the government to investigate what Voss is up to,' said Cassius. 'I sensed his interest in you, after the events in the museum, and I tried to protect you – warning you against telling anyone about it and burning your school records.'

'Why burn my records?' said Bert.

Cassius glanced at his feet. 'I'll get to that part in a moment,' he said. 'I managed to sneak aboard Voss's airship before he set out in pursuit of you. There was little the government could do officially to stop him – he was, after all, chasing after a pirate ship that had attacked his prison. But I knew that if I stayed close, I might be able to gather what his real plans were.'

Bert couldn't argue with the facts and felt himself weakening towards Cassius a little. But he was still wary of letting a government lawman into their midst. 'And?' he said.

'From what I can tell, Voss wants the power of the spirit to activate some ancient weapon,' he said. 'It's something magical, obviously. And something very big.'

Bert nodded. Cassius's story matched the hints he'd gathered back at the prison. 'He needed Norton to power something,' he said. 'That was what the doctor was trying to say.'

'Norton?' said Cassius.

'That's what he's calling the spirit,' explained the Professor. 'Bert was under the illusion it was one of his school friends, apparently. But it was invisible to us the whole time.'

'Fascinating,' said Cassius.

Bert felt tears welling up in his eyes. It was hard enough losing Norton. Hearing someone else explain the situation made him feel foolish and alone in his grief.

'Do you think Norton will help him?' said Cassius.

'Voss said he doesn't need the spirit to help willingly,' said Bert. 'Whatever he's planning, he's already got what he needs by trapping Norton in that dark crystal.'

Cassius sighed. 'This is bad,' he said. 'There won't be time to get help.'

Bert felt the need to act fast. 'We have to go after Voss,' he said. 'Norton's in trouble. I know that Voss is going to do something terrible. If we wait, there won't be a chance to save him.'

'You're in no state to travel,' said Cassius.

Bert shook his head. 'I feel worse the further I get from Norton,' he said. 'I can feel it.' He pointed to his chest. 'If he gets too far away, I don't think I'll recover.'

'Are you sure?' said the Professor.

Bert nodded weakly.

The Professor stood up. 'Then I'll get the crew ready to fly,' he said. 'We'll make for Tralvere. Hopefully we can work out what Voss is planning along the way.'

'Thank you,' said Cassius.

The Professor patted Bert on the shoulder and

hurried out of the room. He was left sitting across from the quæstor. He found it hard to feel any warmth for the man who had chased them across Penvellyn, and he still had questions. 'Why did you burn my records?' he said.

Cassius looked uneasy. 'I'm not sure you should hear it now.'

Bert had a sinking feeling. He dreaded to think what could be so serious that the quæstor needed to protect him from it. 'Tell me,' he said. 'I'm strong enough.'

'All right,' said Cassius, reluctantly. He looked at his hands, as if unsure how to proceed. 'There was an old family that lived in Penvellyn. They used to be very powerful, in their own way, but they were also very wise, and very generous. Their importance meant they were friends with the royal family, even though they had supported the government when the king was forced to hand over his power.' Cassius pulled a face. 'We don't need to go into all of that history now. The important thing is, when one of the family's young daughters was visiting the royal palace she met a young prince, who was very lonely. The young girl took pity on him and treated him as a friend. This boy spent more and more time at the house of the family, exploring the building and playing in the gardens, and he seemed much happier. He loved their library, which was filled with books about distant lands and histories of the old times in Ferenor –

when mages and monsters still roamed and magic could be harnessed. But though he was welcome in the house, there was one rule – he was not to go to the attic, where they kept their oldest family treasures. To begin with, this seemed like a very reasonable rule to the boy, and it never occurred to him to break it.

'But then one day he saw the little girl playing with some other children and he grew very jealous. He thought, why shouldn't he go up into the attic if he was truly welcome? He wanted to be more special than any of the other visitors. He was vain like that. So, he went up, and he found . . . well, things that he couldn't explain. Mechanisms that worked on their own.'

Bert realized what Cassius was getting at. 'Magic?' he said.

'Magic,' said Cassius. 'Artefacts from Ferenor.'

'Were the family mages?' said Bert.

'No,' said Cassius. 'There really haven't been mages for two hundred years, Bert – that much of what the government tells people is true. But there were once. And from what we've seen, it seems as if there is at least one in the world again today.'

Bert shook his head. He didn't believe he could claim to be a mage. He'd thought of magic as a curse since the moment he'd seen it. And he had pushed Norton away and made him feel unwanted, when he was only trying to help.

'I don't have to go on,' said Cassius.

'No,' said Bert. 'I want to hear.'

Cassius shifted in his seat. 'This family traced its origins back to Ferenor, from a time when there were mages, and had persevered some magical objects through the generations. It was one of these objects – I'm not sure which exactly – which drew the boy's attention. He went over to it and placed his hand on it. And something terrible happened to him. When he woke, his arm was gone and he was in horrible pain. The family found him and got him the medical attention he needed. But the king was furious and would never forgive their household. The boy tried to tell his father that it was a magical accident, but no one would listen to him – they thought that he was just making up a story to conceal his own foolishness. After a long time, the boy grew to hate the family that had welcomed him into their house. He told himself that everything that had happened was their fault, and plotted his revenge.'

Bert could sense Cassius hesitating. 'How do you know all this?' he asked.

'I've been investigating it for a long time,' said Cassius, 'back from when I very first joined the quæstors. It has taken a lot of work to piece it all together.'

'And to be clear – this boy is Voss?'

'Of course,' said Cassius.

'I see,' said Bert. It was hard to imagine Voss was ever young.

Cassius sighed. 'When Voss had grown and become a young man – a respected leader – he finally brought his revenge to life. This is when I first started investigating his actions. There was an attack on the family's home. Their house was burnt down. The family were killed, even their servants. It was blamed on bandits, but no one ever found the people who did it.'

Bert felt a chill. 'What happened to the girl?'

Cassius looked grave. 'She disappeared, too,' he said. He hesitated again. 'There was a rumour that she escaped with her child, and hid in the ratway in the factory district.'

A sudden realization began to take hold of Bert. He remembered how familiar the ratway had seemed when he'd fled there with the Professor. He heard, distantly, a woman's voice, telling him it would be all right and huddling with him in the darkness.

'Voss found her,' said Cassius. 'She died trying to lead him away from her hideout – from the child.' He put a hand on Bert's shoulder. 'I'm telling you this because when I saw your notes, I recognized something odd in the circumstances of your arrival at the school, Bert.'

Bert felt his stomach sink. 'There was a man who brought me there,' he said. 'I can't remember anything before that. There are only flashes sometimes.'

'You were very young,' said Cassius. 'And it must have been very traumatic for you.' His voice grew faint. 'I thought you should know.'

'You knew this all along?' said Bert. 'You could have told me at the school.'

'I – I wanted to protect you,' said Cassius.

Bert shook his head. With no one else to lash out at, his anger was focused on the quæstor. He felt as if he'd been betrayed. 'You lied to me?' he said. He knew that he didn't have the energy to bear the shock right now. His arms began to shake. He found it hard to focus. 'I'm not just part of some investigation,' he said. 'This was my family. And they're all gone.'

'I'm sorry,' said Cassius.

The door opened. 'What's he doing here?' said Finch, gesturing at Bert.

Bert heard her voice from far away. He felt a wave of pain and closed his eyes. The weakness was taking hold of him again. He couldn't find the strength to speak.

'We need to get him back to bed,' said Cassius. 'It was stupid of me.'

Bert felt himself being carried from the warmth of the fire. His head was heavy. He wanted to protest, but the shock and the pain were too much. He sank into the darkness.

Chapter 16

H e could hear voices as he lay on the bed. Some of them sounded familiar – like Finch and the Professor – but others were strange and frightening. Sometimes he opened his eyes and saw the wicker on the ceiling. His vision blurred, and he fought the urge to sleep.

Hermatrude dabbed at his brow with a wet cloth. He could feel the cold of the water trickling down his face but he was too weak to thank her.

'He's very weak,' she said. 'I think he's in for a rough night.'

'I thought he said he was better?' said Finch.

'No,' said Hermatrude. 'I'm afraid not, child.'

The feeling of hollowness grew until Bert felt like he was no longer lying in the bed at all. It seemed once again as if he was floating outside of his body. He could hear an airship's engine, but he could only see a deep blue haze. 'Where am I?' he said.

'Don't worry,' said Norton, appearing through the haze. 'You're not really here. You're just, sort of, seeing where I am.' He sat beside Bert, looking bored as usual.

'Norton,' said Bert. 'Let's get out of here.'

'I can't,' said Norton. 'And I can't talk for long either. It takes a lot of energy to keep you here, and I need to save a little bit, you know – in case there's a chance to help.'

'But are you all right?' said Bert. 'Are you hurt?'

Norton shrugged. 'I'm not great,' he said. 'You know how it is.'

'But what's happening?' said Bert.

'I'm in an old castle, hovering in the clouds. That's where Voss has taken me.'

'A castle?' said Bert.

Norton nodded. 'There's a weapon here, Bert. It's very dangerous.'

Bert was still confused. He remembered the painting he'd seen in Voss's vault at the bank. 'How can there be a castle in the clouds?' he said. 'It's not possible.'

'Well, it is,' said Norton. 'And it's miserable. Let me show you.'

Bert felt the floating sensation again and his vision changed. He saw Voss's airship travelling through the clouds at night. The soldiers were busy setting up something on deck.

A bright light suddenly shone from the bow of the ship, reaching out like a pointing finger. Bert recalled the designs for lanterns that he'd seen in the museum, and later in the vault at the bank. This beam was clearly the result of the prince's experiments.

The light passed over the cloud until it came to a tall wisp of white vapours. Then something strange happened. When the light hit the vapours, the mist changed. Suddenly, it transformed into the stonework of a tower. The light moved further, and more towers appeared through the darkness. A whole castle was hovering in the sky, revealing itself wherever the light fell.

'Are you getting that?' said Norton. 'Do you see?'

'I do,' said Bert. 'But I don't understand.'

'Only a magic light will reveal it,' said Norton. 'Like your hand. Or special crystals. Or the sphere that Voss has trapped me inside. That's the only way to clear the mists.'

Bert shook his head. 'How do I find it?'

'It's over Tralvere,' said Norton. 'Just like the quæstor said.'

Bert felt a faint hope stirring inside. He knew that

Norton had to be telling him this for a reason. 'Is there time to stop Voss?' he said.

'Well, you don't have to,' said Norton. 'But if you don't we'll both die and I'll end up being converted into energy.' He shrugged. 'I wouldn't recommend it.'

Bert couldn't help smiling. Even after everything that had happened, Norton still seemed like his old friend from school. For the first time, he considered the way Norton had deceived him. 'Why didn't you tell me who you were?' he said. 'I would have believed you.'

'I don't know,' said Norton. 'It's sort of the rules. Spirits can't tell mages what to do. They just, sort of, hang around with them, and share their powers for a while until it's time to leave.' His voice was growing fainter. 'I'm sorry, Bert. I can't talk any more.'

'Wait,' said Bert.

'Find me here,' said Norton. 'We'll be stronger together.'

There was a flash. Norton vanished into the blue haze.

'Norton?' said Bert. He felt panicked. 'I can still save you, can't I?' He stared through the haze and waited, but there was no reply. A bright light filled his vision.

He could feel that he was waking up.

Bert opened his eyes and struggled to sit up on the bedsheets. 'Finch,' he said. The room had grown dark while he'd been resting. There was a candle flickering in the corner.

'What's wrong?' said Finch. She sat close by. Her hands rested on a book and her eyes looked red. There was no one else in the room. 'Are you all right?'

'I saw something,' he said.

'What are you talking about?' said Finch.

Bert felt strength returning to his limbs. He felt that there was still a chance to help Norton. He fought against the urge to lie back and began to gather his strength.

'What's going on?' said Finch.

'I know where Voss is heading,' said Bert. His head felt clearer now that he had a sense of purpose again. 'We have to head for the clouds over Tralvere,' he said, speaking quickly, in case the dream faded. 'That's where Norton is. I think there's still time to stop Voss.'

'Are you sure about this?' said Finch.

'Go and get the others,' he said. 'I'll explain.'

Finch hurried away and returned with Cassius and the Professor. It didn't take him long to describe the dream. He could tell that the two men were listening intently.

'Can we trust this?' said the Professor.

'I have a connection with Norton,' Bert said. 'Sometimes I can see what he sees. If he showed me that vision, I know I can trust it. Everything else he's shown me was real.'

'But he deceived you about his identity,' said the Professor.

Bert winced. He didn't feel like Norton had lied to him, the way the Professor seemed to think. It was just that Norton hadn't bothered to reveal what he really was.

Cassius nodded thoughtfully. 'Everything that Bert has said fits with the facts we've pieced together. We know that we need to act quickly. This is by far our best lead.'

'Yes, it all fits, I suppose,' said the Professor, grudgingly. He scratched his chin. 'But I've certainly never seen any old castles floating in the sky.'

'Norton explained that,' said Bert. 'You need magic light to see it. Otherwise it looks like regular cloud. He said something about crystals and the light from my hand.'

Finch looked eager. 'I'll go and tell Hermatrude,' she said. 'She knows all about this kind of thing. Maybe she can fix something together for us.' She left the room.

'Did he mention the weapon?' said Cassius.

Bert thought back over Norton's words. 'He said he was going to be converted to energy, but I don't understand why, or why this castle is so dangerous.'

The door creaked and Finch returned with Hermatrude.

'I think I might know,' said Hermatrude. She looked

at the Professor. 'You more than anyone should be familiar with it. You named your ship after it. The *Lugalbanda*. The castle in the sky. It was said to house a staff of lightning – the cause of great destruction.'

The Professor sighed. 'We only called it that because it sounded good,' he said. 'I never actually thought the castle existed. Let alone that it would still be there today.'

'But do you think it could be true?' said Cassius.

'It would explain why Voss wants it so badly,' said Bert. 'He kept talking about wanting real power – the kind of power that would let him rule the country again.'

The Professor looked troubled. 'Well, you know the old saying,' he said. '"Stranger things happen in Ferenor". I'd better go and prepare the crew. It's almost dawn.'

Cassius loitered for a moment after the Professor had left, as if he wanted to say something too. But he couldn't seem to find the words. He nodded to Bert, and headed out.

Finch remained with Bert. A band of light peeked under the curtains. There were birds singing outside. 'Cassius told me about your mother,' said Finch.

Bert nodded. 'It's all right,' he said. 'It's just the shock of it, more than anything. And the sense that I was lied to. I don't think it's really sunk in yet.'

'You know,' said Finch. 'It's not Cassius's fault.'

Bert couldn't meet her gaze. He knew that he should

be grateful for the help of the quæstor. But he couldn't change his feelings. 'It just seems like bad things happen when he's around,' he said. 'I don't know how to explain it. He's obviously been investigating what happened to my family. But I still feel like there's something he's not telling me.'

They were both silent for a while. The airship engine rumbled outside. The Professor was clearly preparing to fly. Finch seemed to be deep in thought.

'You know,' she said. 'I sort of enjoyed being back at school with you for a while. It felt like I was normal, you know, talking with the other children.'

Bert shook his head. 'You're crazy,' he said. He could tell she was serious. It had never occurred to him that someone so adventurous could feel lonely. But thinking about school reminded him of Norton again, and his guilt seemed to overwhelm him.

'You really miss him, don't you?' said Finch.

Bert nodded. 'It's so strange to think you've never met him,' he said. 'For me, it's like he was always there, on this whole adventure with us. And back at school too. He was . . .' He trailed off before he could say 'my best friend'. The words brought tears to his eyes.

'I understand,' said Finch. She gave Bert a quick hug and then headed for the door. It was clear that she was feeling emotional too. 'Are you ready for this, Bert?' she said.

Bert nodded and wiped his face. 'I'm ready,' he said. He pushed away the bedsheets, and reached for his flight jacket. 'At least, I hope I am,' he muttered to himself.

Hermatrude put up a strong protest against the idea of Bert leaving his bed. But the Professor and Cassius were quickly convinced, especially when they saw the change in him.

Ever since his dream, Bert had felt stronger. And he knew from what Norton had said that following Voss would make him stronger still. He could walk, and think clearly again. But he couldn't sense any magic in his hand and a hollow feeling in his chest still pained him.

With Finch's help, he headed outside and saw his surroundings for the first time. Hermatrude's house was a kind of burrow built into the side of a grassy mound, with tall chimneys sticking out. It lay in a meadow overlooking a gleaming blue lake. Over the lake towered the looming peaks of the Sethera Mountains, where Bert fancied he still saw a fire smouldering. The airship hovered by the lake's shore, with its guy ropes staked into the earth.

Finch led Bert over the meadow. The light was growing in the east and the stars were fading. Bert looked up at the *Lugalbanda*, tethered to the ground in front of the shimmering lake. It looked magical in the dawn light, like an ancient dragon waiting to take to the skies.

The Professor and Cassius were talking by the lakeside.

'We'll have to take on Voss's airship,' said Cassius. 'The *Vulture* isn't your average Penvellyn-built vessel. She's bristling with guns, and packed with amphor engines. She'll be able to outgun and outrun anything you can do with the *Lugalbanda*.'

'I still have a few tricks up my sleeve,' said the Professor.

Cassius didn't look reassured. 'And the boy?'

The Professor seemed to waver. 'If what he says about the bond between him and the spirit is true, it's a greater risk to leave him here,' he said. 'I suppose he'll have to come.'

'I think you're right,' said Cassius. He glanced over and seemed to notice Bert for the first time. 'Are you sure you're up for this, Bert?' he asked. 'You were very ill—'

'I'm fine,' interrupted Bert. 'I just want to save Norton.'

The crew quickly got to work firing up the ship's engines and raising the gasbag to its maximum level. Soon the *Lugalbanda* was pulling against its tethers. Finch helped Bert into a sling and he was hauled up on deck, still feeling dizzy but trying not to show it. He looked down at the purplish mark on his hand and wrapped the bandages tighter.

'Roberts,' called Hermatrude from below.

Bert looked over the side and saw that she was carrying a heavy-looking bag stuffed with odd metal objects. He couldn't even begin to guess their purpose.

'New equipment,' said Hermatrude. 'Grand volume smoke bombs, high tortion support wires, self-fastening grapples and a new aerial escape device. If you're interested.'

'Anything for this magic cloud business?' said the Professor.

Hermatrude held up a glowing canister. 'I've cobbled together some crystal emitters that might do the job,' she said. 'You can fire them like flares if you need to.'

The Professor shouted his thanks and lowered a rope for the supplies. Finch went to wave Hermatrude goodbye. 'We'll try to bring you something nice,' she yelled.

Hermatrude shook her head. 'If this magic weapon is as evil as it sounds, I think I'd rather you didn't bring me any part of it.' She stepped away from the billowing exhaust of the engine. 'Good luck to you all, and especially to you, Bert. You're a boy of great spirit.'

Bert smiled at the double meaning of Hermatrude's words. The guy ropes were untied, and the last crewmen scrambled back on deck. Sunlight split the haze and turned the lake a dazzling silver as the ship rose into the sky. The engines rumbled, and they headed north.

Chapter 17

....

Astrange feeling took hold of Bert as he stood at the front of the airship, watching the wild forests of Ferenor passing below. The scar on his palm flickered for a moment then grew cold. He wasn't sure what it meant, but it filled him with foreboding. He was worried about Norton.

The lake shrank from view and the Sethera Mountains grew hazy in the distance. The Professor briefed the crew. Some looked confused, but all were eager to proceed. Apparently, Tralvere was well-known for being permanently cloudy – another promising sign.

Bert was about to join the Professor at the ship's wheel when something strange happened. His vision filled with blue light and he heard a chilling voice.

'The process begins,' said Prince Voss.

Bert shuddered. The vision faded but the fear didn't. He sensed that Voss had reached his goal. That meant Norton was in danger.

He felt a sudden pain and clutched his chest. The sensation travelled from the mark on his hand towards his heart. He sank down and leant against the ship's railing.

Cassius approached. 'Are you all right, Bert?'

Bert tried to steady himself. 'I'm fine,' he said. 'It's just . . . I think I heard something from Norton.' He felt another jolt of pain. 'I think Voss has already found the weapon.'

'Sit down,' said Cassius. He took Bert's shoulder and helped him rest against the side of the hull. Finch came running over. 'He's had a vision,' explained Cassius.

'Of Voss?' asked Finch.

Bert nodded and tried to hide his discomfort.

'I'm going to get medicine,' said Finch. 'Don't move until I get back.'

Bert began to protest but she was already running to the deck hatch. The pain had lessened but he still had the terrible sense of emptiness. It seemed to surround his heart. Worst of all, he knew that whatever was happening to him was happening to Norton.

'We'll get to him,' said Cassius. 'Just hold on.'

Bert looked at the quæstor. He'd avoided speaking with the man while they'd been making their preparations. It was hard to shake off his wariness.

'I'm sorry I couldn't be more open with you before,' said Cassius. 'I had a lot of trouble keeping my position secret from Voss. If I'd seemed too sympathetic . . .'

'It's all right,' said Bert.

Finch returned carrying a box with some bottles in it. She began to sort through the various concoctions, reading the labels in a way that wasn't very reassuring. Bert noticed that whoever had built the box had misspelt 'Surgeon' as 'Sergon'.

Finch popped open a bottle and frowned at the label. 'I suppose this will have to do,' she said. 'I can't say I'm much of a doctor though. Are you always this much trouble?'

'Not until I met you,' said Bert.

'You're forgetting I've seen your school records,' said Cassius.

Bert gave a weak smile. He recalled something that was bothering him. 'That night you burnt my records,' he said. 'Why did you have to throw Freston out of the window?'

Cassius frowned. 'What?'

Finch cleared her throat. '*Actually*, that was me,' she

said. 'The boy kept snooping around when I was trying to talk to you, so I thought I might give him a scare.' She looked down. 'Anyway, I think you should take some of this,' she said, holding out a bottle.

Bert took the bottle. 'You threw him out of a window?'

Finch shrugged. 'I made sure he didn't fall.'

Cassius appeared quietly amused.

It was odd to talk about school. So little time had passed, but already it seemed like a distant memory. Everything he used to worry about seemed so trivial.

He drank the medicine to please Finch but he already felt as if the pain had passed. He stood up and tested his legs, feeling somewhat stronger. He could sense that they were getting closer to Norton. His palm was tingling slightly, as if the magic was returning.

Cassius looked as if he was about to say something more when they were interrupted by a call from the look-out. Strange rock formations appeared over the horizon. They were like three short spires and they reached up from a bare hillside. Bert had never seen anything like it.

'The Towers of Wheldrake,' said Finch. 'Once we pass those we'll be over the plains of Tralvere. Then we'll see what this cloud business is all about, Bert.'

Bert nodded. He felt excited, but apprehensive too. There was a chance he could be wrong. If there was no sign of Voss, or this strange castle, he wouldn't know where to turn.

Cassius moved away as the crew began to adjust the fin-like sails, and the Professor took hold of the wheel. It was clear that they were preparing for action.

'I want to help too,' said Bert.

Finch shook her head. She brought over the bag of tricks that Hermatrude had given them and began to sort through it. She took out some armour and a few brass canisters. Then she came to a trio of lumpy backpacks. She didn't appear to be familiar with them.

'Are these things safe?' said Bert.

'I think so,' said Finch. She peeked inside one of the bags. 'I think this is the new aerial escape device that Hermatrude mentioned. But I can't figure out how it works exactly. There's a strap here, and a toggle that seems to pull out. It says "pull when falling".' She opened a pamphlet that was packed amongst the inventions and began to read in silence.

Bert was pleased to see how eager she was and how prepared the crew seemed. But his thoughts kept drifting to Norton and the hollowness in his chest. He felt helpless. He remembered Norton reaching out to him as the dark crystal slid across the hold of the *Erebus*.

He gritted his teeth and looked over the horizon. The forests had faded away into a flat plain with a brown river running through it. It looked like a wasteland. There was thick cloud cover in every direction and it made the day seem dark and foreboding.

'Airship, two points north!' yelled the lookout.

A ripple of excitement swept over the deck. Bert felt strangely relieved at the sight of the approaching adversary. If the airship was coming to intercept them, that confirmed his vision. But it meant danger too. Everyone waited for the Professor's orders.

The Professor kept his expression level. 'Very good,' he yelled in reply. He gazed at the approaching speck over the horizon. For a moment, he appeared to consider their options. Then he nodded calmly. 'Make course to intercept them,' he said. 'Full speed ahead.'

'I hope you're not actually thinking of fighting that thing head on,' said Cassius, as the Professor passed the wheel to Mr Peel. Bert followed them over the deck.

'I'd appreciate it if you didn't question me in front of my crew,' said the Professor. He led them past the row of cannons, checking the charges as he went. 'Load the mortar with Hermatrude's crystal emitters,' he said to a nearby crewman. 'We need to be prepared.' He turned to Finch. 'You and Bert can do a special job for me. I want all the timber we can spare brought on deck and wrapped in the old gasbag cloth. And a couple of amphor barrels too, for good measure.'

Finch looked confused for a moment. Then she gave a smile. 'I'll get them right away,' she said. She beckoned for Bert to follow her and headed below.

'What's this about?' said Bert. 'Are they just getting us out of the way?' He followed her down the ladder to the main gangway of the lower deck.

They passed through a tight corridor. The planks creaked and the amphor lamps flickered as the engine rose in power. It was like being in a rickety house in a storm.

'No, he's definitely got a plan,' said Finch. They came to a heavy door. She knocked open the latch and beckoned for Bert to follow her inside.

The hold was dark and crammed with all kinds of supplies – everything from spare hammocks to barrels of preserved food. It had an odd woodland smell. Bert helped Finch rummage through the shelves until they'd gathered a good pile of spare timber.

'I still don't understand,' said Bert.

Finch climbed a ladder and knocked on the ceiling of the hold. A hatch slid open above and a crewman lowered down a winch for them to attach their bundle.

'Is this for some kind of trick?' Bert asked.

Finch nodded encouragingly. 'What does this look like?'

Bert frowned. 'A load of junk.'

'And what would you think if you saw a load of

burning junk falling from the sky? If you'd just seen an airship heading down into the clouds, for example?'

Bert began to see what she was getting at. 'I suppose I'd think the ship had exploded,' he said. He smiled despite himself. 'That's amazing,' he said. 'Have you done it before?'

'Well, not yet,' said Finch, grinning. 'There's only one drawback, I suppose.'

'What's that?' said Bert.

'Not actually getting blown up in the process,' she said. She finished tying the ropes and gave the signal for the crewmen to haul the junk up on deck.

They followed it up and closed the hatch.

Bert was shocked to see how quickly the enemy ship had closed with them. It had a dark grey gasbag with lower hull painted red. Even at this distance he could tell it was bigger than their ship and it was clearly built to fight. Rows of cannons poked from its sides.

Bert walked to where Cassius and the Professor were standing.

'That's the *Vulture* all right,' said Cassius. He passed a viewing telescope back to the Professor. 'They were obviously prepared for us. I wonder if Voss is aboard.'

'Ever been in a real air battle?' said the Professor.

'Only the odd skirmish with pirates,' said Cassius with a wry smile.

The Professor laughed. 'Well, enjoy the change of view.' He turned to Bert and Finch, and nodded appreciatively. 'Well done with the wreckage. I'll need you two to perform some of the theatre during the fighting too. We're going to put some of Hermatrude's new smoke bombs in barrels at the back of the ship. You can open them when it seems appropriate.'

Finch nodded eagerly. Bert tried to mimic her enthusiasm. Like most Penvellyn school children, he had read stories about air battles when he was younger. He knew that airships could blast each other to pieces in a matter of moments and that they could easily get disabled in mid-air and boarded too. He never imagined he'd be in a battle himself.

'Who's the enemy captain?' the Professor asked Cassius.

'Captain Stokes,' said Cassius.

'What's he like?' said Finch.

'Ruthless,' said Cassius. 'He almost killed five of his own men on the way out here with his strict rules and cruel punishments. He'll stop at nothing to win.'

'I see,' said the Professor. 'Then it will be a fair fight.' He turned back to the ship's wheel and yelled: 'Mr Peel, if you could bring us just above the clouds, that would do nicely.'

'Right you are, sir,' called the haggard man at the wheel.

The ship began to rise. Bert saw the *Vulture* immediately adjusting its course to meet them. They would break through the clouds at the same time. At the speed they were currently travelling, it seemed likely the ships would meet just as they surfaced.

'All right men,' said the Professor, as he walked along the row of cannons. 'When we crest this cloud canopy, they're going to be right in front of us. We only need to last a few volleys to make our plan work, and that means we're going to get to fire some shots of our own, too. Make every cannonball count, and show them that we're not some band of posers.'

Some of the more elaborately dressed crewmen looked uncertainly at each other during the Professor's speech. One man self-consciously touched the feathers in his hat.

The Professor corrected himself. 'I mean, it's all right if we are posers,' he said. 'But we can also fight, you know, when we need to. And look wonderful doing it.'

A more confident cheer went up from the men. In the same moment, the first mists of the cloudbank fell upon them. Bert caught a final glimpse of the *Vulture* heading right at them, with its hull looming. Then the deck was bathed in white. The cloud vapours swirled like rain over the gasbag and pattered on the deck. The men squinted over their gun barrels.

'Steady,' yelled the Professor. 'We'll be out any moment.'

Cassius nudged Bert. 'Make sure to stay low,' he said.

Bert nodded. Finch was already leading him through the mist towards the back of the ship, where the smoke barrels had been stored. His heart beat loudly in his chest.

He heard a deeper rumbling growing over the sound of their own engine. The clouds were clearing. Finch grabbed his hand and led him faster. 'Hurry!' she yelled.

Bert could feel the vibrations of the other ship's engine shaking in his bones. He glanced over his shoulder and saw a dark shape materializing through the white vapours.

The deck burst into clear sky and the hull of the *Vulture* emerged through the clouds beside them. A line of guns bore down through the haze.

Bert saw the crew of the *Lugalbanda* staring over their own cannons; the Professor standing by the ship's wheel, Cassius gazing defiantly at the opposing deck.

'Get down!' shouted Finch.

Bert threw himself into the side of the ship's hull just in time. There was a huge ripple of explosions and the deck disappeared in a cloud of grey smoke. A yell of pain went up from one of the gun crews and splinters burst from the hull. A rigging rope fell where Bert and Finch were crouching. Bert coughed through the smell of gunpowder and looked around. In a matter of moments, the deck had been transformed into a scene of chaos. There were gaping holes in the side of the hull and fires smouldering in the rigging. The men were shouting to one another.

Through the haze, he saw the enemy airship had almost passed.

'Fire!' yelled the Professor.

The *Lugalbanda*'s guns blared out in response. Another burst of smoke shot out into the slipstream and Bert saw flashes and puffs of impacts on the *Vulture*'s deck. It seemed impossible that the airships could fling so much metal at one another and yet keep flying. The *Vulture* shuddered under the force of the blows as it glided swiftly behind them.

'The smoke,' said Finch. 'Now.'

Bert saw the barrels she was pointing to. She kicked one of them over and indicated that he should do the same. He heaved the barrel down fast as he could.

The containers popped open, and a dense cloud of smoke billowed out, making it look as if the whole rear of the ship was on fire. Bert coughed and staggered back.

'Well done,' said the Professor, appearing beside them. He squinted through the smoke. Bert followed his gaze to the opposing airship. It had flown by at speed, but it was already turning to chase them. It looked like a prowling shark as it skimmed over the clouds.

'This is our only chance to make the trick work,' said the Professor. He took hold of the ship's wheel and angled them downwards, falling rapidly towards the cloud cover.

Bert's stomach lurched at the speed of the drop.

'Come on,' said Finch. She led him over the shattered planks and fallen ropes to the wreckage that was wrapped in the spare gasbag. The crewmen gathered. A man with a long match lit the fuses on a pair of explosive barrels and rolled them up with the rest of the junk.

'When do we throw it?' asked Bert.

'Now!' yelled the Professor. As he spoke the airship sank into the clouds and the deck was bathed in white once again. The wind whistled over the rigging.

Bert's hands moved blindly over the parcel of wreckage, helping the crew to force it over the side of the hull. Finch ran up and give it a final kick.

The bundle plunged into the white abyss. The Professor levelled off the ship and cut the engine and for a few moments they sailed in silence. A huge explosion split the air below.

Some of the crew muttered nervously.

'Everyone stay quiet,' whispered Finch.

A low rumbling approached. The noise built until it seemed like it was coming from all around them. There was no way of telling if the trick had worked.

'Remain calm,' whispered the Professor.

Bert felt as if he was in a strange dream. He could barely see his own hand through the white haze. The wet vapours clung to his skin. Everyone around him waited in tense silence as the rumbling surrounded them and made their teeth rattle in their heads.

Bert held his breath and tried to get his bearings. Suddenly a shadow moved over the cover just below them. He could hear soldiers calling to one another.

'It went down,' yelled a stern voice. 'Give me a sighting.'

'I saw a smoke trail leading this way, sir,' called a voice in a reply. 'There was an explosion. No sign of anything up here. It's likely they fell apart beneath us.'

'Let's look at the wreckage,' yelled another voice.

'Aye, aye, sir,' called the men in reply.

The engine grew louder and the *Vulture* began to descend. Bert let out a long breath. He could still barely see the faces around him but he could sense their relief.

'Take us to manoeuvring power, Mr Peel,' said the Professor quietly. 'Minimum speed until we're out of earshot. We don't want to give them cause for alarm.'

'Yes, sir,' said Peel. The crew pattered over the deck and the ship began to move again. A few crewmen were being treated for splinter injuries and a fire smouldered in the rigging, but otherwise they'd come through remarkably unscathed. As the sound of the other airship quickly faded to nothing, Bert could still sense apprehension in the voices of the men.

Finch seemed to read his mind. 'It might have worked for now,' she said. 'But we can't be sure that they'll be fooled for long. If they chase us again, we'll be in for a real fight.'

Chapter 18

Now that the immediate fear of the opposing airship had passed, Bert began to consider the task ahead of them. His instincts told him that they were still heading in the right direction and he was feeling stronger by the minute. But he wasn't sure how they could find their objective while they sailed through the cloud. He wasn't even sure what to look for.

The Professor appeared through the mist. 'It looks like we're going to get a clear pass at the skies of Tralvere. Can you give us any hints?'

Bert was daunted by so much responsibility. But he could *feel* he was getting closer to Norton. They were on the right course. 'There were towers in the clouds,' he said. 'They looked like regular mist from a distance. But that's just a screen. They're solid enough.'

'Anything else?' said the Professor.

'Just the light,' said Bert. 'When the light from Voss's ship fell on them, it showed what they really were.' He shook his head. 'I suppose that's the best I can do.'

'We're doing fine, Bert,' said the Professor. 'This is what Hermatrude's crystal emitters are for. If she's right, they'll reveal the structure, just like Voss's light did.'

'But how will we see through this haze?' said Bert.

'We'll have to trust our luck for now,' said the Professor. 'It's too dangerous to reveal ourselves with the *Vulture* around. That wreckage won't fool them for long. In the meantime, you should take a break. You've done well.' He smiled and walked back to the ship's wheel.

Bert had no intention of sitting down and waiting. He wasn't convinced that the lookouts would be able to spot the odd clouds from his description and the hollow feeling was growing in his chest. He couldn't miss his chance to save Norton. His gaze wandered to the rigging. The gasbag overhead seemed to reach almost to the top of the cloud. There was a long periscope on deck nearby. A plan began to form. He spotted Finch heading past the cannons.

'Finch,' he said. 'I need to get on top of that gasbag.'

Finch looked surprised. 'Are you sure?'

Bert gave what he hoped was a confident nod. 'We're running out of time,' he said. 'I'm the only one that knows what those clouds look like. I need to spot them myself.'

Finch glanced around to see if anyone was watching. 'Well, they can't complain once we're up there,' she said. She grabbed the periscope and a pair of ropes with hooks on the end and led Bert over to the rigging. The haze helped mask their movements.

Cassius was walking close by. 'What's going on?' he said.

Bert's heard sank. He couldn't let the quæstor stop him now.

'Quickly,' said Finch. 'You go up first.'

Bert was already running. He gave one last look at the deck then climbed the rigging as fast as he could. The slipstream hit him as soon as he left the cover of the deck and the sound of the wind filled his ears. There was an overwhelming temptation to look down.

'Here,' yelled Finch. She appeared beside him and wrapped a rope around his waist. She attached a hook at the end of the rope on to a line that hung down over their heads.

'What do we do now?' said Bert. He couldn't see a way to get from the rigging on to the underside of the balloon. There was only that stray line hanging in the haze.

To his horror, Finch kicked off from the rigging and let herself hang in empty space. 'It's all right,' she shouted. 'Trust the safety line. We'll climb it together.'

Bert felt a wave of dread sweep over him. But there was no time to hesitate. He let go of the rigging and kicked off. His stomach lurched as he dangled over the side of the balloon.

'Climb,' said Finch. She pointed to a section of knotted rope that led up the line, all the way over the top of the balloon. He didn't need much encouragement. With Finch beside him, he scrambled up as fast as he could, wincing as the sharp gusts battered him.

When they reached the top of the balloon he was shaking heavily but still in one piece. He caught his breath for a moment. From his seat on top of the balloon he saw breaks in the cloud cover and caught flashes of brilliant sunlight. Finch passed him the long tube of the periscope. She helped to steady the device while Bert looked into it. He cast his gaze to the north.

To begin with he couldn't seeing anything remarkable about the skyline ahead of him. But as he focused, he became aware of an odd prickling sensation in his palm as he looked to the north-east. He wasn't sure if it was because he was getting closer to Norton or because of the presence of some other inspiration, but it seemed that he had gained a little more of his power. He raised his right hand. A weak blast emanated from his scar. The energy travelled like a flare across the sky ahead until it passed a high swirl of mist. The clouds flickered as the light passed by and the mist grew more solid for a moment. Bert stared in wonder as the turret of a castle appeared. He almost dropped the periscope in surprise. 'I can see it,' he gasped.

'Where?' said Finch.

Bert passed her the periscope and forced another flicker of light to emanate from his palm. It was much weaker this time but Finch still registered its effect.

'That's incredible,' she said, in obvious wonder. 'There are towers, just floating there.'

Bert took the periscope back from her and looked again. He could tell now that there were a whole host of misty columns floating over the bank of cloud cover. It seemed unbelievable, but if his instincts were right, each one of those columns was a part of the same floating structure.

'It must be huge,' said Finch. She shook her head in disbelief. 'I have to get down and tell my father to change course. I'll help you down afterwards.'

'I'm fine,' said Bert. 'I should stay and keep a lookout.'

Finch looked uneasy. 'Just don't unclip your safety harness,' she said. She hurried over the surface of the gasbag and disappeared down the rigging.

Bert couldn't help feeling a pang of concern. The wind was biting, even through his thick clothes, and the gasbag seemed fragile as it rippled beneath him.

But he felt stronger with each moment. He knew that meant they were getting closer to Norton. It was as if the energy he'd lost was returning to him. He was still gazing in wonder at the columns ahead when he heard a noise that made him flinch.

A deep rumbling followed them through the cloud cover.

'Airship behind!' yelled a lookout from below.

A blast of smoke split the cloud behind them.

The *Lugalbanda* lurched like a startled animal as the engine burst into life. The *Vulture* had clearly spotted them. It was gaining rapidly. Bert clung on to the gasbag and checked that his hook was still attached to the safety line. The wind buffeted him.

He knew that he was in a precarious position if the fighting started again, but the prospect of climbing back down the rigging without help made him hesitate.

There was an explosion close by and a burst of smoke.

The *Vulture* fired at them with its chase cannons. Another shot rang out and a burst blossomed out just over the gasbag. Bert winced as the ship shook.

He tried to crawl over the rocking surface of the gasbag but a sudden pain forced him to stop. The ache around his heart had returned. The hollowness grew and a terrible coldness flowed over his chest. He saw a flash of blue light and dark shadows. 'Norton,' he muttered. He could sense his friend was in serious trouble. Whatever Voss was doing was harming him. He remembered what Norton had said about being killed and made into energy.

The *Lugalbanda* rocked on a swell of air and the cloud cover disappeared for a moment. Bert could see the column-like mist ahead. They had almost reached it.

Another explosion nearly sent him tumbling.

The rumble of the *Vulture* jarred through his mind. Explosions burst in regular patterns now, all around the sides of the ship. He heard the shrapnel whistling through the air. Another twinge of hollowness gripped him and he sank down, holding his chest.

'Norton, hold on,' he muttered.

He knew he needed to get down on to the deck. He tried to ignore the blasts of cannon fire and focus on his footing, but as he crawled towards the side of the balloon a new impulse took hold. They had almost reached the spot where he'd seen the first tower. He sensed that he didn't have much time left if he was going to save Norton. If he could somehow get on to the structure, it might be his best chance of reaching the dark crystal and stopping Voss completing his plan.

A powerful searchlight ignited at the front of the

pursuing ship. It shone over the clouds. Under its beam, a whole curtain of mist seemed to vanish and revealed a network of towers and walkways. Even in his apprehension, Bert couldn't help a feeling of wonder at the scene. They appeared to be almost at the heart of the gigantic floating castle. The *Vulture* had clearly activated the light to prevent a collision with the structure, but they had also shown the pirates the way.

There was a sudden impact and the ship lurched drunkenly.

Bert was thrown on to his hands and knees. He saw the gasbag of the *Vulture* suddenly sail by and bank away from them. Its searchlight disappeared. The floating structures that had been there a moment ago turned back into cloud. The *Lugalbanda* seemed to have frozen in mid-air.

'We've struck something,' yelled a voice from below.

The crewman's words mirrored Bert's own thoughts. The ship hung practically motionless, despite the roar of its engine. The nose of the gasbag was buried in the haze. Bert held out his hand and a weak light shone from his palm. The mists parted as the magical light fell on them and revealed the face of a castle wall, just as he'd expected. There was a stone walkway right beside him. It was almost within his reach – the side of the gasbag scraped against it.

A desperate thrill passed over him. They had reached the castle and that meant Norton was somewhere nearby. All he had to do was get inside.

'Adjust course,' yelled the Professor's voice below. 'And will someone for goodness sake get Bert down from the balloon. He's not some cursed ship's mascot.'

The ship lurched again. The balloon slipped back from the cloud.

Bert felt a rush of panic. He couldn't hesitate now and there was no time to explain. He unclipped from the safety line and ran, making straight for the cloud ahead.

'Bert!' yelled Cassius from close by. 'Come down from there.'

Bert couldn't afford to look back. He jumped.

For a sickening moment he saw clear sky, before he plunged into the thin vapours. Then he suddenly crunched against something brittle. He realized he wasn't falling any more.

He gasped and looked around. He was on solid ground, sort of. His legs had sunk into the crumbly white structure that seemed to make up the walkway in the cloud. Thinner white vapours swirled around him. They seemed to rise from the stone's surface like a cloak. The airship gasbag still hovered close by. He called out but his voice was lost to the rumbling engine.

A shadow fell over him and he caught sight of the

Vulture returning for another attack. 'Bert,' called Cassius, from somewhere close by. 'Where are you?'

Bert wasn't sure how to reply. 'Over here,' he yelled.

He could hear the Professor's voice shouting orders, even over the rumbling engines. 'Fire the crystal emitters! We need to find a way of manoeuvring!'

There was a sudden flash from the front of the *Lugalbanda*'s deck and a cascade of blinding lights shone overhead. Bert blinked at the sharpness of the glow. As his vision cleared, he clearly saw the layout of the castle. Ghostly white towers and turrets rose all around. Ahead, across a series of walkways, there was one tower that was bigger than the rest. He knew Voss would be there. Somehow he was certain that the weapon was there too.

The rumbling grew louder and the *Vulture* came into view, skirting the edge of a nearby tower. Bert could see that the *Lugalbanda* was drifting too far away for anyone to reach him. He wouldn't be able to count on the help of the crew. But the fear of what was happening to Norton, and the hollowness in his chest, drove him onwards. 'I'm all right,' he yelled, hoping that Cassius, or someone on the deck, might hear him. 'I'm on the cloud.'

The *Lugalbanda* climbed rapidly, and turned its side to the *Vulture*. There was a sudden flurry of explosions between the two ships and the air filled with grey smoke. Some of the shots hit the castle and stone tumbled through the mists. The walkway shook beneath Bert.

He felt a pang of concern for his friends, but at the same moment he realized the precariousness of his position. The structure he was standing on kept shaking under the force of the explosions and a stray cannonball burst through the surface nearby. Fissures spread over the stone from the impact. It dawned on him, violently, that he was standing on something at least two hundred years old – a floating ruin in the clouds. For all he knew it might drop at any moment.

A crack split the walkway beside him. He staggered to his feet and began to run. From the corner of his eye he saw the edge of the walkway falling away like a pile of sand.

The airships fired again. It seemed like the whole place was disintegrating now. He made a desperate dash towards the centre of the slope, but it was too late.

The ground gave way beneath his feet. He fell through a layer of cloud, grasping at the brittle structure and bringing it crumbling down around him. Then everything went white.

For a moment, Bert was disorientated. He'd landed at the bottom of a crumbling slope on another narrow walkway that hovered over what seemed to be empty space. The flares of the crystals still illuminated the outlines of the castle around him, but it was clear that they wouldn't last much longer. They flickered in the haze and the stonework faded in and out of the mist.

He flinched as a voice called out to him.

'Bert,' said Cassius. 'Are you down there?'

'I'm here,' yelled Bert.

Cassius appeared, running down the crumbling slope. He took hold of Bert's hand. 'Are you all right?' he said. 'Are you injured?'

Bert was struck by the concern in the man's voice. He felt a flood of gratitude to the quæstor. In his heart, he didn't believe he could face Voss alone, and he could sense now that the prince was nearby. Norton seemed to be calling out to him.

'Let's move,' said Cassius. 'The flares are running out.'

Bert remembered his powers. 'I can see without them,' he said. He held up his hand. The light from his palm was weak, but it was enough to part the haze ahead of them and reveal the true path, even as the flares sank from view. 'I think it's this way,' he said, gesturing ahead.

They made slow progress over the ghostly ruins. The mist faded ahead of them and closed behind, so that their patch of walkway was the only clear ground.

He couldn't even see the airships any more. They passed a strange statue of a flying creature with frightening eyes. He could just make out a large archway ahead.

'I don't like this,' said Cassius. 'Voss could be hiding anywhere.'

'He'll need a light too,' said Bert. 'We'll have some warning.'

The clouds parted momentarily and he caught a glimpse of the airships. He was relieved to see that the *Lugalbanda* was still intact. There was another flurry of cannon fire and something crashed above them. A tower crumbled through the thick cloud.

'Look out!' yelled Cassius. He grabbed Bert as the ground sank from beneath their feet. They fell for a moment and landed in a heap on a black stone floor.

When they came to rest, Bert realized that the quæstor had been winded by the fall. 'Are you all right?' Bert asked.

Cassius nodded. 'Just a knock,' he said.

'Thank you,' said Bert. He felt a pang of guilt for not having trusted the quæstor before. 'You risked a lot to come here. I don't know what I'd have done alone.'

Cassius smiled. 'You're doing fine,' he said. 'What is this place?'

Bert looked around. A weak reflected light illuminated a black stone corridor lined with mirrors. They stuck at jagged angles through the walls, like veins of crystal, with only the odd black pillar to break the glare.

'At least we can see our way now,' said Bert.

They edged along the corridor, with Cassius peering around cautiously. The effect of the mirrors was like a fun fair. Bert found it hard to keep his bearings.

Cassius shook his head. 'I feel like I'm in an old fairy tale,' he said. 'I always used to love stories about Ferenor when I was a child. Now look at me.'

Bert saw a flicker of amusement in the man's eyes. He remembered his own eagerness for adventure when he was small. He hadn't imagined it would be like this.

'What's that?' said Cassius, back on alert.

A greenish light spilt out from an archway ahead of them. Each time the light flickered their surroundings showed clearly for a moment. Bert could see that the corridor opened out into a wider room ahead. There were more carvings of winged figures. Their faces had a hungry, wicked look about them. They reminded Bert unpleasantly of Prince Voss.

As he stared at the green light he felt a dawning terror. 'This is it,' he whispered to Cassius. 'That light is coming from the dark crystal. This is where Norton is trapped.'

Cassius nodded. 'Stay behind me,' he said.

As they drew closer, Bert saw that the room was split by more reflective surfaces. When the light flashed, he glimpsed a large domed ceiling, but it faded quickly into mist.

'Stay low,' said Cassius. He led them to the opening

of the room, treading softly. By now Bert could almost hear Norton calling to him. The green light was dizzying.

A flicker of movement caught his eye and a bright flare slid along the floor. It came to rest beside them. It took him a moment to realize the cause.

'Look out,' cried Cassius.

Bert felt the quæstor barrel into him and heard a gunshot. He landed against a pillar beside the entranceway. Cassius landed heavily beside him.

The light went out almost as suddenly as it had appeared and the mists closed in. Bert couldn't focus to get the power from his hand. He fumbled blindly.

'Cassius?' he said.

There was no reply.

'Cassius, are you there?'

He heard a weak gasp from near his feet and held up his palm, focusing the power. A weak light emanated from his scar.

The mist parted and he saw to his horror that Cassius was slumped against the wall, breathing heavily. He was clutching his chest. There was blood on his hands.

'Voss,' said Cassius. He winced. 'He's in the mist ahead.'

Bert placed his hand over Cassius's and tried to put pressure on the wound. He realized that Cassius was staring at him. A look of peace passed over the man's face.

'You have your mother's eyes,' he said through a wince. 'I'm sorry I couldn't be there for you.'

It took a moment for Bert to register what Cassius was saying. He gripped the man's hand tighter and shook away his surprise. 'Hold on,' he said. 'I'll find some way to help you.'

Cassius moved his head weakly. 'It's all right.'

'You knew my mother?' asked Bert. The realization of who Cassius really was began to sink in. He knew that the quæstor had been hiding something, but hadn't dreamt it was this.

Cassius let out a long breath. His face darkened. 'I was away when it happened,' he said. 'I was always away back then. When I found out what had happened to her, I had to hide you. She had wiped your memory. It was a final attempt to keep you safe, I suppose. Even if it meant you forgetting us.' He winced and gripped Bert's arm. 'You can't let him win,' he said.

'I can help you,' said Bert. He unwrapped the bandage from his palm and tried to press it against Cassius's wound. His hands were shaking.

Cassius's expression grew vacant, as if his mind was somewhere far away. He seemed to look beyond Bert. 'It's all right,' he said. 'It won't always be scary. I promise.'

Bert felt tears on his cheeks. He remembered the man in the cloak who had brought him to the school. 'It was you,' he said. He struggled to speak. 'You're my father.'

Cassius' gaze lost all focus. He slumped lower against the wall. Bert clutched his hand tighter and called out to him, but it was clear that he was gone.

Chapter 19

Bert was frozen for what seemed like a long time. The glow from his palm faded and the mists closed in. He was shaken out of his grief when a new light appeared nearby. The silhouette of a large man strode towards him. He let go of Cassius's hand and picked up the man's sword. It felt heavier than the weapons he'd used before, but he managed to hold it on guard.

'Voss!' he yelled into the mist, with an anger he'd never felt before

The silhouette drew closer, then stopped. The mists parted and the green light flickered to show Voss standing in the archway, holding a sword.

'You're too late,' said Voss. He gestured towards the dark crystal, inserted in a staff at the centre of the large room behind him. It was the source of the light. 'Your spirit is already powering the device. Soon it will be fully consumed.' He continued to stride towards Bert. 'Once it is stored inside that staff, there will be nothing left of your friend but lightning – lightning that I can use to destroy whatever I choose.' He snorted. 'Starting with your pirate friends.'

Bert barely registered Voss's voice. He was still thinking of Cassius, and who he really was. The prince's ambitions seemed petty in comparison.

Voss looked blankly at him. 'But there is one small piece of business that I need to resolve,' he added. 'In this new world, there can be no one to rival my power. I will be the only wielder of magic.' He charged with surprising speed and swung his sword.

Bert met his attack swiftly but the force of the blow knocked his guard high. The man shifted his footing and fired a kick at Bert's stomach.

Bert had no chance to dodge. He took the blow and flew back against the mirrored wall, then rolled towards the archway.

Voss watched him intently. 'You are not without skill,' he said.

Bert backed into the large room. He could feel how

close Norton was as he paced towards the flickering green light. He felt strength returning to his hand, just like when he had faced Freston in the competition back at school. An angry red glow burnt in his palm. The mist hovered at his feet.

Voss charged again and made a thrusting attack.

Bert was ready this time.

Their swords met with a flash of sparks. In the same instant, he deftly changed his guard and jabbed at his adversary.

Voss snarled and staggered back, holding his face.

Bert used the opportunity to back closer towards the green light. The closer he got to it, the more his power seemed to return. He was certain Norton was trapped there.

'You are a mistake,' hissed Voss. 'You were never meant to take what I had created.' The light from the staff flickered for a moment and Voss disappeared into the mist.

Bert gasped and looked around in confusion. The clouds closed in. He turned to run but a shadow blocked his path.

He flinched as a stinging pain erupted in his shoulder, and struck wildly.

Voss was hit. He snarled again in rage and grabbed Bert's sword in his metal hand.

There was a screech of rending steel. The sword broke and sprang from Bert's grasp. Voss tossed the pieces into the mist and kicked Bert back along the floor.

Bert was winded and stunned, but Voss was clearly injured too. He staggered a few paces away from Bert and seemed unable to hold up his sword.

Bert had landed beside the green glow. He could see the dark crystal trapped inside a glass sphere placed on top of a metal staff. The staff appeared to be made of gold and was covered in strange black writing. A coil of green energy flickered from the sphere to the staff.

He felt new power burning inside.

'It's over,' said Voss, his eyes locked on Bert. 'This world is mine, little mage.' He drew his pistol from his belt and took aim. 'Go and join your spirit friend.'

Time seemed to slow for Bert. He saw the pistol hammer click and a puff of smoke shoot from the firing cap. But at the same instant he raised his hand and aimed.

A blast of energy shot from his palm. It travelled over the room like an explosion. The floor crumbled into a pit at Voss's feet and a cloud of debris shot into the air.

Voss's bullet seemed to vanish in the wave of energy. The prince gave a scream of pain and disappeared in the chaos of the explosion. His pistol flew from his hand.

When the light flickered again, the prince had vanished. There was a large hole in the floor where he had been standing. The ground was visible far below.

He staggered to his feet and caught his breath. Norton needed him. He could see the light growing stronger around the crystal trapped in the sphere. He couldn't afford to hesitate. He could feel that his friend had almost been lost to the device.

He reached to lift he sphere from the pedestal but a blast of green light struck him and a pain shot through his heart. It was as if some physical force was trying to keep him from taking possession of the crystal. He had to fight the pain to place his hand on the glass. His thoughts grew hazy. For a moment, he saw a flash of the night when he'd arrived at his school. There was a foggy street ahead of him and a voice saying: 'I wouldn't want him to be scared of the darkness.' He saw Cassius's face hovering close by and a young woman looking down on him, telling him she was sorry – telling him to hide.

He forced away the memories, then smashed the glass of the sphere with his hand. The crystal burnt under his fingertip. A green light enveloped him.

Suddenly the world seemed to disappear. He plunged into a sea of blue light and deep shadows. There were shapes that looked like people but they were hard to make out. He felt like they were closing in on him. 'Norton!' he yelled. He reached out his hand.

A strong grasp clutched his own.

'Hold on, Norton,' yelled Bert.

He strained as hard as he could. The light and shadows faded and he surfaced again in the real world. He fell back on the floor with the dark crystal in his hand.

There was no sign of Norton. The ceiling looked cold and bare. His heart seemed to beat very slowly. He couldn't feel the presence of his friend any more.

Footsteps echoed across the room. To Bert's horror, Voss reappeared. He must have been blasted clear of the hole and hidden in the confusion of the debris. He was clearly injured and limping, but he had his sword in hand. He edged around the hole in the floor and approached shakily. 'You,' he said, pointing his metal finger at Bert. 'What have you done?'

Bert frowned in confusion. He didn't understand what the prince meant. He was certain that he had lost Norton. There was nothing left for him to ruin.

A shadow moved through the mist behind the prince.

'Give me that,' yelled Voss, as he snatched the crystal from Bert's grasp. 'I want you to fix it, do you hear me?' he said. 'I need you to use your power.'

The shadow drew closer, and a familiar face appeared through the mist. 'Hello,' said Norton.

Voss flinched away. He held the crystal out towards Norton, but this time it didn't seem to have any power over him. Flashes of light appeared beneath the prince's fingertips, and Bert noticed for the first time that its light had changed from green to a deep blue.

Norton stood staring at the prince.

'Watch out, Norton,' said Bert.

'It's all right,' said Norton.

The prince swiped at Norton with his sword, but it did nothing. His hands were shaking. He held up the crystal again. 'Get away,' he yelled.

'I'd let go of that if I were you,' said Norton. 'It's dangerous.'

Voss held the crystal tighter. A blue light emanated from its surface. 'Get back where you belong,' he snarled.

Norton didn't move. 'I tried to warn you,' he said.

Bands of energy crackled over Voss's hand. He staggered back. The crystal slipped through his grip and landed on the floor.

His body seemed to grow transparent.

'What did you do to me?' he said, with a look of terror.

'Nothing,' said Norton.

Voss turned and made a grab for Bert but by now the prince's body had almost vanished. His metal arm fell to the floor with a thump. His face seemed to age.

There was a flash of light and he vanished completely. The crystal flickered and went out. It fell towards the edge of the hole that Bert had blasted in the floor.

Bert reached for it on instinct.

'No,' said Norton.

Bert paused. 'Are you sure?'

'I think he's better in there,' said Norton. 'Let him go.' The room shook. The crystal slid into the hole and tumbled into space. They watched as it plunged from sight.

'Well, that's that,' said Norton. He helped Bert to stand and cast a light around them to cut through the mist. The structure didn't seem to be doing well after Bert had removed the sphere from the pedestal. The walls shook and he could hear ominous crumbling sounds, but for the moment he was too exhausted to pay them much attention. He followed Norton and they sat together on the edge of the hole in the floor, letting their feet dangle.

'Are you going to be all right?' asked Bert.

'I think so,' said Norton. 'Thank you for your help. I wouldn't have been happy in this thing.' As he spoke there was a rumble and the structure shook violently. 'I mean on the one hand, there are fewer people to bother you, but I imagine it would get boring.'

'Is this thing going to crash?' said Bert.

'I hadn't really considered it,' said Norton. 'But probably, yes.'

Bert's heart sank. He was exhausted and there was no way of getting off the structure. They might have beaten

Voss but it seemed like a hollow victory. He began to worry about the Professor and Finch – whether they had got away from the *Vulture*.

'I'm glad to see you again, Bert,' said Norton.

Bert smiled, despite his worries. 'Me too.'

A new sound caught his attention. Footsteps echoed from the corridor and Finch appeared. 'Bert!' she yelled. She was holding a glowing crystal emitter. 'I knew you'd landed here.' She sprinted over to join him by the hole. The roof began to crumble.

Bert got up to meet her. 'Are you all right?' he said. He felt choked by emotion. 'What happened?'

'We won,' Finch replied, with a grin. 'We sent one of Hermatrude's precision shells straight through their engine block. They had to go down for a crash landing.'

'You shouldn't have come here,' said Bert.

'Don't be a complete clod,' said Finch. 'How's the . . . you know . . . Norton thing.'

'Nice of someone to ask,' said Norton.

'We saved him,' said Bert. 'But Cassius . . .'

He trailed off and glanced towards the corridor.

'I saw,' said Finch. 'I'm sorry, Bert, but we've got to leave.' She tossed a package into his arms. It was light and it looked like a backpack, with straps that fastened around the waist.

'What is this?' said Bert.

'It's the aerial escape device,' said Finch. 'Don't you remember?'

'But you never figured out how to use it.'

Finch waved her hand dismissively. 'It's fine,' she said, looking down through the hole. 'I'm pretty sure this will give us a clear drop. My father is bringing the ship back around.'

A huge section of the roof fell away beside them and the floor began to split. Bert looked at Norton and felt an irrational pang of fear at the thought that Finch hadn't brought an escape device for him. Norton seemed to read his mind. 'I'll catch up,' he said.

Bert nodded, and looked down over the drop.

Finch grabbed his hand. 'With me,' she said.

'Right,' said Bert. He held tighter and looked back at the corridor where he had left Cassius. He felt a wave of sadness and regret. But he knew the man – his father – was gone.

'Now,' said Finch. She leapt over the edge.

Bert dropped with her. The remains of Lugalbanda Castle flashed by as they plummeted through the opening. The gap looked like it was closing in.

Bert raised his hand and fired a blast of energy.

They burst out into clear sky.

Finch pulled a cord that was attached to his backpack. He heard a hiss above him, and saw something white shoot up from his back. There was a dull thud.

He looked up and saw a circle of white material hovering over his head like an umbrella. It had arrested his fall. He was floating down to earth.

Finch opened her device later, but she was safe too. He could hear her shouting to him but he couldn't make out the words over the sound of the wind.

A large chunk of white stone flashed by and shot towards the ground. Bert looked up in alarm and saw that the whole of the floating ruin was coming down.

'Finch,' he yelled. 'Look out.'

She yelled some reply but he knew that his warning had made no difference. There was no way of controlling his descent and the structure was clearly too big to avoid.

A rumbling sound grew over the wind. Bert glanced over his shoulder and saw for the first time that the *Lugalbanda* was sailing towards them. It was streaming smoke and looked as if it had been battered by storms, but it was still flying.

The gasbag was almost under him.

Finch's voice somehow carried over the din: 'Land at the centre!'

Bert clutched the strings and tried to guide his fall. He saw Finch touch down and figures rushing to her aid. Another large piece of debris fell by, almost hitting the ship, and more was on the way. His feet touched down on the gasbag and a strong grip attached a safety line around his waist. He looked up to see the concerned face of the Professor.

'Cassius?' asked the Professor.

Bert shook his head sadly.

'I'm sorry, Bert,' he said. He gave the order for full speed and the ship jolted forwards. The castle cast a shadow over them as it fell.

The crewmen braced, and yelled warnings.

Bert reached his palm upwards. A cold energy flowed through his body. He felt a shockwave burst from his palm, trying to hold the structure back, but it didn't seem to do anything.

He raised his hand again.

The ruin suddenly froze above them.

Bert looked up in confusion. He could see a black figure floating in mid-air below the ruins. Norton was holding the crumbling structure back. The airship powered out from the shadow just in time. There was a deep rumble and the whole castle mass fell again, screaming down towards the plains.

'Come on,' said the Professor. He hurried Finch and Bert over the side of the rigging. The ruin struck the ground and a huge explosion blossomed from the impact.

They reached the deck just as the shockwave hit. The ship listed wildly before righting itself. Bert found his feet and saw that the Professor and Finch were safe.

He looked back to where Norton had been floating but he couldn't see anything. He remembered the way his friend had collapsed after fighting the skeletons. A sinking feeling took hold of him. 'Norton,' he yelled. He looked around the deck. The crewmen stared back at him blankly. He searched over their faces, looking for some sign of his friend returning.

There was no reply.

'Is he here?' said Finch. 'Did you rescue him?'

Bert shook his head. He couldn't sense his friend nearby. He ran to the edge of the hull and looked back at the debris cloud where the ruin had struck, searching for some reassurance.

A shadow fell on the deck beside him.

'What are we looking at?' said Norton.

Bert let out a long breath and a curse. He put his arms around his friend, and laughed in relief. He remained like that for some time, even when he became aware that the crew were staring. Of course, they couldn't see what he was so happy about. But by now he didn't care.

Epilogue

....

A golden light fell across the *Lugalbanda*'s deck as they skimmed the tree tops. Two days had passed since the battle – two days of exchanging tales and repairing the damage. Bert felt a clinging sadness at the memory of Cassius, and a deep regret for not having spoken with him more. There were still so many questions about who he was and where he had come from. He managed to piece together a little of the story by talking with the Professor, but not much.

'Your family were famous,' said the Professor. 'Your father was a member of another noble family, I believe, from far-off lands to the west. He disappeared on the same night as your family's home was burnt. Never seen again. Now we know that he continued to live, under a new identity.'

'I still don't understand why he left me,' said Bert.

The Professor sighed. 'I can't look into Cassius's heart, Bert. But I can see why he thought you were safer alone, at that school. Voss is no easy adversary to trick and his spies were everywhere, even in those days. Cassius had to keep his real identity completely secret to become a quæstor. And I suppose what he told you was true – he spent years investigating the circumstances of your family's murder, in search for justice. It must have been very hard.'

Bert swallowed. It was difficult to speak about Cassius's real identity without losing himself to sadness. But he was pleased he had known his father, if only for a short time.

He also tried to speak to Norton about what to do now, and whether he was still in danger, but his spirit friend was strangely evasive. He told Bert that they should head east until they found a particular ruin. Now, in the quiet of evening, they had finally reached their destination.

'Structures ahead,' yelled a lookout.

Bert went to the front of the ship with Finch and stood on the edge of the hull, holding the rigging. The breeze stirred his hair. Ahead he could see stone ruins rising over the tree canopy. They passed a vast archway covered in climbing plants and startled a flight of birds.

'Is this where you meant, Norton?' he asked.

Norton gave a casual glance overboard and nodded. The crew were mostly used to Bert talking to thin air by now, although the accordion player still looked a little nervous when Bert passed on Norton's song requests.

'I just wish they weren't always about death,' the man complained.

'There's a good landing ground there,' said the Professor, as he brought the ship lower. 'I want ground crews to set up a perimeter. Then we can stretch our legs.'

The sounds of the engine ceased and the airship glided the last stretch. It seemed peaceful enough below. The crewmen threw ballast overboard and fastened the guy ropes.

'All secure, sir,' said Mr Peel.

'Very good,' said the Professor. He went over the rope ladder and gestured for Bert and Finch to follow. Soon they were standing in a clearing in what appeared to be an ancient courtyard. There were crumbling walls all around them and flagstones peeking through the weeds.

'All right,' said the Professor. 'Lead on, Bert.'

Bert looked to Norton and his friend began to saunter casually through the ruins, looking this way and that and pointing out the odd feature to Bert as he went.

'You've been here before?' asked Bert.

'A long time ago,' replied Norton. He walked up a set of crumbling steps and brought them to a castle-like wall. There was an empty doorway ahead of them. 'In here,' he said. He glanced at the Professor and Finch. 'You should tell them there's some treasure in that ruin over there.' He indicated a particularly dilapidated mound of stonework.

'Really?' said Bert. He knew that the Professor and Finch would be thrilled. As he relayed the information it was obvious that they intended to excavate straight away.

'Are you coming too, Bert?' said Finch.

Norton shook his head.

'Not just yet,' said Bert.

'All right,' said Finch. 'We'll be close if you need us.'

The Professor was beaming. 'You explore if you want, Bert. But remember, this is a very important historical site. If you see anything that looks valuable, put it in your pocket.'

Bert assured them that he would do just that.

'This way,' said Norton. He passed through the archway and brought Bert into a large open ruin with an impressive set of steps leading to what looked like a glass throne.

'What is this place?' said Bert in amazement.

Norton moved slowly to the seat. 'This is where the king used to sit,' he said, simply.

Bert paused. He could hear the sadness in his friend's voice. It hadn't occurred to him that Norton was so old. He wondered at how much he must have seen.

'You know all the history of Ferenor?' said Bert.

'Well, I've met a lot of mages,' said Norton. 'But I've never had such a big adventure.' He spoke in a matter-of-fact way. 'It used to be common for us to reach out into your world and find a person to share our powers with. We sort of gain energy from it too. It makes us new again.' He looked thoughtful. 'You know, Bert – I think you would have enjoyed this place.'

Bert nodded. 'I think I would have too,' he said. He remembered how Finch had talked about places in Ferenor that made you feel as if you had stepped back in time. He could sense it now. The stones seemed to radiate past conversations and forgotten souls.

Norton fell silent for a while.

Bert wasn't sure how to ask, but looking around the ruins brought an obvious question to mind. 'What happened to the people that used to live here?'

'Well,' said Norton. 'You know how it is.'

Bert shook his head. 'I really don't.'

Norton seemed resigned. 'To begin with this land did well under magic. But once people got used to power, well, they weren't very nice. Spirits like me would come to this world briefly for each normal exchange. But even so, it was clear that something was going wrong. War broke out. People were less happy each time we appeared and they were getting meaner to each other. So, we stopped giving our power to the people of Ferenor as freely as we once had.' He shook his head. 'Of course they weren't happy. Some of them made creations like that dark crystal Voss carried. And things like the staff in the floating castle. Those things unmade spirits like me, just to take our power. After a while, there weren't many spirits left. There was nothing for it – we had to stop passing through the mirrors. If not, they would have destroyed all of us.'

Bert frowned. It had never occurred to him, even after what he'd seen of Voss's artefacts, that the mages had caused their own downfall in such a cruel way. He thought of the bond he had with Norton. He felt sick at the idea that someone would corrupt it for power.

'Then Voss started trying to force a spirit into your world,' said Norton. 'I knew I had to do something.' He yawned. 'Not that I was very happy about it. It was only when I saw you on the other side that I thought there might be a chance of putting things right. I mean, I could see you had the potential of a great air mage. And they were always the best, in my opinion. But I had to be sure you could handle some power on your own first. It's sort of part of the process.'

'Air mage?'

'I forget you don't know about these things,' said Norton. 'They're one of the rarest kind, as it happens. There haven't really been many since the world began.'

Bert was delighted. He supposed that explained why none of the mage powers he'd read about fitted with his own. 'So you chose me?' he said. 'It wasn't an accident?'

Norton shook his head. 'It wasn't an accident,' he said. 'In fact, in a way, we've always been together, although it's sort of hard to explain. In a way, we sort of share a spirit.' He looked a little sheepish. 'When you were at the museum, I realized that was the best chance to show you what Voss was up to, so I sent you through the mirror.' He looked down at his feet. 'Sorry about that.'

Bert laughed despite himself. It seemed silly to have Norton apologize to him after all they had been through. But he still had questions. 'Did you burn the museum too?'

'Well, I knew that I couldn't leave that mirror where people could tamper with it,' said Norton. 'And they had a few other very dangerous things there too – like the automatons.' He winced and rubbed his forehead. 'The automaton wars were just the worst, Bert.'

Bert found it hard to take in. He still saw Norton as his lazy friend from school, despite everything that he had discovered. It was hard to picture him taking part in grand events. The sun was falling low and the ruins grew darker and more malevolent.

'There were good mages too,' said Norton. 'Even in the last days of Ferenor. It was hard for us to abandon them. But a few must have made the journey to Penvellyn before the final wars wiped out this land completely. You certainly remind me of some of them.'

Bert hesitated. 'Cassius said I'm descended from mages.'

'It would make sense,' said Norton. He sat down in the glass seat as the first stars began to appear overhead. 'But I suppose these are things you'll have to find out on your own.'

There was something about the way he said the words that made Bert pause. He began to get a sinking feeling. 'Why have you brought me here?' he said.

'I thought it was a good place to say goodbye,' said Norton.

Bert winced. 'But you've just come here – to my world,' he said.

Norton looked around glumly. 'I've been here long enough, this time,' he said. 'If I stay now my power will drain and it could harm both of us. That's just the way it is.'

'I have so many questions,' said Bert.

'I doubt I can explain much now,' said Norton. His face was set in its customary miserable way, so that it was hard to tell if he was feeling any worse than usual. 'But I suppose there's time to ask one more thing, if you really think it would help.'

Bert swallowed, and tried to keep down his sadness.

He sensed somehow that this had to happen, but it was still painful. 'All right, Norton,' he said. 'One last question.'

'What is it?'

'Did you enjoy your time here?'

Moonlight fell on Norton's seat. He stared back for a long moment and the ghost of a smile passed over his features. As the next shadow fell, he was gone.

Bert walked back out into the moonlit courtyard. He felt strangely whole again, even though he was sad about Norton leaving. And he was glad he hadn't wasted his last moment on some selfish query. He looked down at his hand and saw that the scar seemed to have healed a little already. He couldn't feel the pull of magic inside him any more either.

He supposed that meant his powers had vanished. Norton had destroyed the dangerous magical artefacts at the museum, put an end to Voss and his evil ambitions, and helped rid the world of the castle in the sky. It wouldn't make sense to leave a mage wandering around – even if they were friends.

Bert went towards the glow of a lantern where the Professor and Finch were excavating the mound of stone. They didn't look particularly happy either.

Finch noticed him first. 'What's wrong?' she asked.

'He left,' said Bert. 'He wanted to explain a few things to me before he went, but, you know, he had to leave.' He spoke quickly so he wouldn't get too emotional.

Finch knocked some of the dust and dirt off her hands and came to give him a hug. 'I'm sorry, Bert,' she said. 'I suppose that means no more magic for you?'

Bert nodded. 'I suppose.'

'Well,' said the Professor, appearing from a hole in the rock pile. 'You're just in time to help us search for treasure. I've been digging for some time now and I've only found rock.'

Bert had an inkling he knew what was going on but he wasn't sure how to put it. 'I'm afraid there might not be treasure down there after all,' he said, feeling awkward.

'What do you mean?' said the Professor.

Bert cleared his throat. 'Norton did say it was there,' he explained. 'But based on past conversations, I think that it might be his idea of a joke.'

The Professor's face darkened. 'You're sure?'

'I think so,' said Bert.

'Right.' The Professor let out a long breath. 'Well, he's got a funny way of showing gratitude, that's all I can say.' He climbed out of the hole and dusted himself down.

Now that Norton was gone, Bert felt troubled about his future. 'Professor,' he said. 'I was wondering. I suppose we've done what we set out to do . . .'

'You're wondering where we're going next?' said the Professor. 'Well, don't worry, Bert. There are plenty of lucrative prospects for a pirate in these lands. We'll talk it over once we're back in the air, but I was thinking we might try and explore to the east of here.'

'Where the basilisks live?' gasped Finch.

'Where they're *supposed* to live,' said the Professor, in an annoyed tone. 'If you ask me, I think they're nothing more than pirate rumours, trying to scare us away from treasure.'

The two of them walked ahead for a moment and Bert was left smiling to himself. Apparently, it had never occurred to the Professor and Finch that they wouldn't keep him aboard once his adventure was over. He was relieved. He took a step forwards and then hesitated. The rock pile had shifted slightly behind him. He turned around and squinted in the darkness. He couldn't see clearly without the lantern.

A silvery light suddenly appeared around him – perhaps it was some lucky break in the clouds – and he stepped closer to peer down into the excavation.

There was something down there all right. He reached out into the darkness with his scarred hand, and heard a dull rumbling sound below. It almost looked as if the rocks were moving of their own accord. He lowered himself into the hole and looked around, still feeling confused.

There was a pile of something shiny lying in bags in the darkness, and lots of gleaming objects. 'Finch! Professor!' he yelled. 'I think you ought to see this.' He picked up one of the bags – it contained dozens of gold coins. Then his smile dropped.

His hand was glowing in the darkness.

He looked at the mark on his palm. A silvery light emanated from it. There was no pain or coldness, and no sense of energy being depleted. But he was definitely using magic.

'What is it?' yelled Finch from the surface. She began to scramble down into the hole, knocking the stones loose as she went. 'Is this another joke?'

'I'm not falling for the same thing twice,' said the Professor.

Bert quickly hid his hand behind his back and closed his palm. He didn't want to shock them and he felt it would be better to explain later, when he had some idea of exactly what was going on. Instead he gestured towards the room and tried not to look too pleased with himself. 'Correct me if I'm wrong, Finch,' he said. 'But I think I just found treasure.'

Acknowledgements

....

The Boy Who Went Magic wouldn't have come to life without the help of some great people. I'd like to say thanks to Sam, without whose thoughts and ideas I'd never have got started; to Callie, for believing someone might want to read it; and to Kesia and everyone at Chicken House for supporting me through its various incarnations. I'd also like to thank my friends at the bookshop for being so dorky about the whole thing. Finally, a big thank you to Jess, for helping every step of the way.

THE SECRET KEEPERS by TRENTON LEE STEWART

A magical watch. A string of secrets. A race against time.

When Reuben discovers an old pocket watch, he soon realizes it has a secret power: fifteen minutes of invisibility. At first he is thrilled with his new treasure, but as one secret leads to another, he finds himself on a dangerous adventure full of curious characters, treacherous traps and breathtaking escapes. Can Reuben outwit the sly villain called The Smoke and his devious defenders the Directions and save his city from a terrible fate?

'There are some genuinely haunting and ingenious moments as the three young heroes combat the villain in his mouldy mansion.'
THE NEW YORK TIMES

Paperback, ISBN 978-1-911077-28-2, £6.99 • ebook, ISBN 978-1-911077-29-9, £6.99